A PHOENIX IN THE BLOOD

Below them was spread the great sprawling mass of the city, thousands of lights glowing like cigarette ends through the darkness.

'It's certainly quite a sight,' he said.

'It makes a perfect ending to the evening.'

'Have you enjoyed it so much?'

'Enjoyed it? If only you realized.' There was a sad intensity in her voice and he tried to see her expression in the dim light thrown up from the dashboard. She looked out over the lights of the city. 'When I get married I'm going to have five children — at least five. And I shan't leave them for a minute — not ever.'

For a moment he was going to reach out to her through the darkness. To tell her that he also had been lonely and that he understood. Instead, he said, 'I'd better get you home,' and he started the engine and drove away.

Also in Arrow by Harry Patterson

TO CATCH A KING
THE SAD WIND FROM THE SEA
THE VALHALLA EXCHANGE

As Jack Higgins

A FINE NIGHT FOR DYING
HELL IS ALWAYS TODAY
TOLL FOR THE BRAVE

A PHOENIX IN THE BLOOD

Harry Patterson

ARROW BOOKS

Arrow Books Limited
17-21 Conway Street, London W1P 6JD

An imprint of the Hutchinson Publishing Group

London Melbourne Sydney Auckland
Johannesburg and agencies throughout
the world

First published by Barrie & Rockliff 1964
Arrow edition 1983

© Henry Patterson 1964

Made and printed in Great Britain
by The Anchor Press Ltd
Tiptree, Essex

ISBN 0 09 931960 8

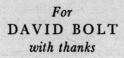

For
DAVID BOLT
with thanks

Chapter One

Jay Williams drove the Land-Rover into the car park at the side of the museum, switched off the engine, and got out and pulled on his greatcoat. He was a tall, brown-skinned man in khaki battledress, the strong angular face and startlingly blue eyes evidence of that mixture of blood so common in Jamaicans. Only the spatulate nose and dark, tightly curling hair, were negroid.

He followed the path round the side of the building to the terrace and stood at the balustrade, hands thrust deep into his pockets, a curiously alien figure, strangely withdrawn. It was as if somehow he had insulated himself from life, as if he stood apart from it.

Beneath him the ground fell steeply away and far below through the mist, he half-glimpsed trees and a lake. From the interior of the museum came the faint strains of a piano and he went through the main door into an impressive Georgian entrance hall lined with mirrors.

A framed poster announced free lunch-time con-certs with Miss Sarah Penfold in a varied programme at the piano. He opened the door and slipped quietly in.

It was a pleasant room, rather long and lined with french windows down one side. He took a seat at the end of a row and gave his attention to Miss Penfold.

At that moment she was half-way through a Schubert sonata. She made no mistakes and her timing was excellent. Unfortunately, she was unable to bring the music to life. Having become aware of this within a matter of seconds, he turned his gaze on the audience.

There were no more than fifteen or twenty people in the hall. A couple of phony-looking intellectuals in velvet jackets and beards were sitting in the front row. They appeared to be enraptured by the performance. Four young students in striped scarves were talking quietly, huddled together by a window. The rest of the audience looked as if they had come in out of the rain.

Jay lit a cigarette and there was a movement beside him. A quiet voice breathed in his ear, "You can't smoke in here. They'll put you out."

He hurriedly extinguished the cigarette and saw that his well-wisher was a schoolgirl sitting two seats away from him. She appeared to be seriously intent on the music.

"Thanks very much," he whispered.

She turned her head, nodded, and turned away again. He was conscious of a strange excitement. She had the most appealing face he had ever seen. He watched her out of the corner of his eye. She was wearing a rather unattractive green school uniform complete with a wide-brimmed felt hat with a band round it in the school colours. On her feet were scuffed brown shoes. There was a briefcase on the floor beside her and she was eating a sandwich with complete lack of self-consciousness.

Miss Penfold was coming to the end of a spirited rendering of a Chopin polonaise. She finished dramatically, hands raised high. As the final notes died away a low-pitched snore sounded from the rear of the room.

Jay turned his head and saw an old gentleman fast asleep in the back row. His eyes met those of the schoolgirl. They both looked hurriedly away and clapped, but the applause sounded thin and feeble in the large room. Miss Penfold left and did not return despite the hearty cries of encore from the bearded gentlemen.

The audience showed no immediate desire to leave. Jay sat there for a few minutes, then decided to go. He walked out on to the terrace and re-lit his cigarette. He stood looking down towards the trees and the lake. On a sudden impulse he descended the steps from the terrace and followed the path down the hill. Five minutes walk brought him to the trees and through them, he could see the water.

The searching wind chased the leaves from among the trees so that they seemed like living things crawling along the path in front of him. He walked on to a wooden jetty that stretched out into the lake and leaned on the railing at the end, trying to pierce the misty curtain of rain that shrouded the far shore.

Through the trees he could see the tower of an old church that seemed half-formed, unreal in the mist. Everything had an air of nostalgic beauty and he was filled with a pleasant sadness.

A hollow booming sounded as someone turned on to the jetty. He did not look round as the steps approached. A voice said, "Hello!" and the schoolgirl who had been sitting near him at the recital, leaned over the railing.

"Did you enjoy the music?" he said.

She shook her head. "I thought it was terrible. Makes one wonder what the academies are turning out these days. What did you think?"

He shrugged. "We shouldn't grumble too much. After all, it was free."

She turned towards him and again he felt that strange, disturbing flutter at the sight of the piquant young face.

"That isn't much of an excuse," she said. "If you set out to entertain people, you should do just that. The money question has nothing to do with it."

"Maybe you have something there, but I wouldn't say it too loudly. A lot of amateur talent would be rather annoyed."

She laughed. "You're right. I'm always putting my foot in it. If only you knew the scrapes I've been in simply from telling the truth."

"Lesson number one," he said. "Always be careful about the truth. It's amazing how people can't stand it."

She smiled again. "How wonderful. I've always thought that, but you're the first person I've met who's agreed with me."

"Do you get to the lunch-time concerts often?"

She shook her head. "My school's too far away. As a rule, I just don't have the time, but today's a half-holiday. I didn't really come for the recital. It's the park I like to see. I love it here in the autumn."

"I must confess I'm impressed," Jay said. "I never expected anything like this in a grimy northern town."

She turned again to look at him. "You haven't been here before? Oh, but it's marvellous. The Corporation bought it as a park and turned the old mansion into a museum. That's where the recital was held."

"Rather a funny place for a museum," he said. "I mean it's a long way from the centre of things."

"You should see it in the summer. It's crammed with people then." A seagull cried harshly as it skimmed the surface of the lake and she looked up and said, "That's what I'd like to be when I die . . . a seagull flying over the water in the rain." She kept her face turned up to the sky and let the rain fall on it. "This is how I like it best. Hardly anyone around. And the rain—I love the rain."

Her eyes were closed in ecstasy and she held up her face until rivulets of moisture ran all over it. There was a vibrant, glowing air to her as though she was straining after life itself and somehow believed the rain could give it to her.

Jay pulled out a handkerchief and said, "Here, mop

your face. It'll be running down your back in a moment."

"But it is," she said with such an expression that he was convulsed with laughter. "Come on, I'll show you round the lake. It's lovely at the far end. The woods run right down to the water's edge and there are some islands with swans and wildfowl."

They walked along the cindery path that skirted the edge and the wind blowing across the water, brought with it the dank, wet smell of rotting leaves.

"That smell," she said. "Isn't it wonderful? Doesn't a day like this make you feel good to be alive?"

He couldn't answer her in words because the words wouldn't come. She was right. It was a wonderful day and it was good to be alive and it had taken this amazing child to make him realize it.

One thing above all that intrigued him was her tremendous awareness of living. Of being one with the wind and the trees, the sky and the rain.

As they came towards the far end of the lake, the rain increased into a heavy downpour. "Come on," she shouted. "We'll get drenched," and took to her heels.

Jay followed her example, but the heavy greatcoat hampered his movements. She was standing in the shelter of a huge beech tree while he was still twenty yards away.

"And men are supposed to be the stronger sex," she said triumphantly.

He opened his greatcoat and took it off to shake the

raindrops from it. "You try sprinting in army boots and a greatcoat. You won't find it so easy."

She was looking at the insignia on his shoulder. "Intelligence Corps?" She seemed impressed. "What are you doing in Rainford?"

"My National Service."

"Aren't you rather old for that?"

"I'm a positive greybeard," he said. "If you must know, I'm twenty-three. I was deferred several years to go to university. My name's Jay Williams and I'm looking for Russian spies."

She laughed and said in an off-hand way," Caroline Grey. But twenty-three isn't old. My grandfather would call you his boy. And there aren't any spies in Rainford. This is a textile town and spies aren't interested in textiles."

She had stopped him cold. For a moment, he could think of nothing to say and then he saw a glint in her eyes and her laughter, hardly contained, bubbled out.

He pulled his greatcoat on and leaned against the trunk of the tree. She pushed a wet tendril of hair away from her eyes. "Did you take a degree?"

He nodded. "A Ph.D."

"Oh, that's very good, isn't it? What did you read?"

"History."

She frowned. "Why?"

He shrugged. "Most people think it's pretty useless. I happen to like it, that's all."

The frown disappeared. "But that's the only worthwhile reason for doing anything."

He was amazed. She was such a peculiar blend of maturity and innocence, of simplicity and wisdom.

She turned away and looked out towards the islands. "What are you going to do when you come out of the army?"

He lit a cigarette and said thoughtfully, "I don't really know. Getting my doctorate was the important thing. What to do with it afterwards just never occurred to me."

"Well it should have. After all, a man has brains for a purpose and obviously you have brains. The thing is to find out your particular purpose and to work at it."

Jay was amused and yet he knew that she was right. She threw pieces of twig into the water with an absorbed look on her face. He wondered how one explained to such a young girl that so often life is not what it should be, but what it is. An awkward phrase, but true nevertheless. A few ducks swirled across the water quacking mournfully, expecting to be fed. She crouched down, her coat dragging in the wet grass, and made comforting noises.

"I wish I hadn't eaten all those sandwiches. These poor things look hungry."

"They get fed all the time." He bent down and pulled her up. "Your coat was getting wet. Pneumonia isn't a pleasant way to leave the world—not for one so young, anyhow."

The candid blue eyes gazed up at him searchingly and he realized that he was still holding her arm. He smiled awkwardly and released her.

"I'm not so young." She turned away. "I'm fifteen. As a matter of fact I'll be sixteen in five months."

The rain at that moment slackened into a light drizzle. "We'd better make a move," he said. "I'll have to put in an appearance back at the unit or they'll send out the search parties."

They walked back along the side of the lake in silence and turned towards the museum. Jay felt awkward because for a fleeting moment, he had become aware of her as a woman.

Caroline seemed unaware of the atmosphere and yet, when he took a quick sideways look at her face, he could have sworn there was a glint of laughter in her eyes again.

They mounted the steps to the car park and Jay stopped in front of the Land-Rover. "This is where I leave you."

"A Land-Rover, how wonderful! I've always wanted a ride in one. Which way are you going?"

"I'm not going into the town centre. I'm going out towards Haxby."

"But how simply marvellous. I live in Haxby. Now I shan't need to waste an hour waiting for a bus."

It was fate, he decided. He opened the door and handed her in. A moment later they turned out of the car park and into the lane that led to the main road.

"I bet I know where you're stationed," she said. "Greystones. They were annoyed, the parish council, when they heard the army was buying the place Everybody thought the village was going to be turned into a sort of garrison town with fights outside The Tall Man on a Saturday night. I must say you've all been very quiet about it. How long have you been here?"

"About a fortnight, but they opened the place two months ago."

"What are you all doing, or is it supposed to be a secret?"

"Not really. You could say we're going to school again."

"What kind of lessons?"

"Russian. Not enough people can speak the language and the army wants to build up a reserve."

She made a face. "I have enough trouble with French and Latin. How long does the course last?"

"I'm not sure. At least nine months, probably longer."

"Good, that means you'll be here for quite some time."

He could think of no suitable reply and concentrated on his driving for the rest of the journey. Just outside Haxby, they came to a pleasant grey-stone house set back from the road in about an acre of garden. She touched his arm and he halted.

She smiled brightly. "It's been awfully nice meeting you."

He nodded. He didn't say anything because he suddenly felt awkward again and wanted to get away as quickly as possible.

She started to get out and paused. "You aren't on duty on Saturday, are you?"

He answered "No" automatically and without thinking.

"Wonderful," she said. "We could go to the Town Hall in Rainford and hear some real piano playing. It's Moura Lympany and the Hallé. I know someone in the booking office. I can get a couple of tickets."

Jay was taken aback and yet he was trapped. There was a forcefulness about her that was impossible to resist. "Well, I suppose . . ."

"Good," she said. "Then that's settled. We may as well have tea in Rainford." She pointed to a bus stop on the other side of the road. "You catch the four o'clock bus in Haxby and I'll get on here."

He had a feeling that the whole thing was completely out of his hands. "All right," he said reluctantly. "See you Saturday."

He eased his foot from the clutch and drove away quickly.

Chapter Two

Half-a-mile along the main road on the other side of Haxby, he turned the Land-Rover into a gateway flanked by massive stone pillars and drove slowly along a gravel drive that cut its way through a dense pine wood. A sharp left turn brought him into a stretch of open parkland and before him lay the house, rooted amongst giant beech trees, grey and ancient and enduring.

He followed the drive around the side and came to a halt in the courtyard at the rear. He switched off the engine, took his small pack from the back seat and entered the kitchen door.

Two disgruntled looking cooks in dirty whites peeled potatoes at the sink. He gave them a brief nod and passed through.

He raced up the service stairs, turned into the main landing and mounted a further flight of stairs. He passed along a narrow corridor and opened the door at the end.

It was a small room with a dormer window and contained two army cots. The man who was lying on one of them, was in his early twenties with hair so fair that it was almost white. His handsome and rather reckless face was saved from weakness by a smile of great natural charm.

He dropped the magazine he was reading. "And where the hell have you been, you old bastard?" he remarked pleasantly.

Jay threw his small pack at the young man's head and discarding his greatcoat, flung himself on the other bed and lit a cigarette.

Dick Kerr smiled amiably. "We thought you'd taken off for foreign parts or something. What happened?"

Jay said, "When I got to Catterick, I reported to M.T. If the Land-Rover had been ready, I'd have been back last night. It wasn't. They let me have it this morning. The M.T. clerk promised to phone through to explain. He must have forgotten."

"Things have been happening here during your absence, big things."

"Come off it, Dick. I only left yesterday morning. Not much could have happened since then."

"Depends how you look at it. At the moment, I'm wondering how long I can remain in hiding from him."

"From whom?"

"Sergeant Grant—our new nursemaid. He's on detachment from a Guards regiment. From my own short experience I'd say they were glad to get rid of him."

"When did he arrive?"

Dick took a cigarette from an elegant leather case.

"It was damned funny really. We had a free study afternoon yesterday, so I put on civvies and went into Rainford in the Jag. I did some shopping, went to a cinema and started back at about five. As I was passing Haxby station, I saw this character in a fancy peaked cap standing on the pavement surrounded by his gear and looking lost. I stopped the car and found he wanted Greystones. I gave him a lift and brought him right up to the house. He called me 'Sir' and hoped he hadn't brought me out of my way. You should have seen his face when I told him I was just a buck private doing the course here!"

"You bloody idiot," Jay said. "When will you learn? He'll feel humiliated now. If he's anything like he sounds, your life is going to be a misery."

Dick chuckled. "*My* life? That's good. You don't know what he's accomplished already. From now on we have drill every day and a sentry box is to be erected at the main gate. That means guard duty in the near future. No more pleasing yourself in the mornings until class starts at nine. Reveille at six and roll call outside."

"Oh, no!" Jay groaned. "Sounds like primary training all over again."

"You haven't heard the best of it. Our lovable sergeant was a commando in his younger days. He mentioned the fact frequently yesterday. He's going to take us for P.T. and unarmed combat lessons, if you please. Says we get soft sitting on our bottoms all day."

"What the hell for?" Jay said. "If we were training

for Field Security work or something I could understand it, but we aren't. Who the hell thought this one up, I wonder?"

"Who do you think? Our revered Colonel Fitzgerald. The War Office must have blessed the day they needed a C.O. for this place. I should imagine he was first choice."

"You've probably got a point there."

Dick shook his head in disgust. "A fine old English gentleman, me boy. Ever wonder how we lost the Empire? Well, he's a walking reason. You and I, we speak well, in fact we're better educated than he is and yet here we are—privates. Because my grandfather was a brewer's drayman with ideas, I have a two thousand pound car parked in the courtyard, and you arrived here by way of Cambridge."

"I think in his heart-of-hearts he still thinks I'm here by some terrible mistake," Jay said. "I'll never forget the involuntary look of horror on his face when he first saw me."

Dick ignored the interruption. "The army of today is beyond his understanding. He can't forgive us for not taking commissions and our presence in the ranks is a blow at the status of officers. We embarrass him by having dinner at The Granby on Sundays. Oh, he'd have been great in the Sudan blazing away at the fuzzy-wuzzies with a Gatling gun."

Jay clapped solemnly. "Quite a speech. I presume that when the day comes, you'll declare openly for the party and hand over your ill-gotten gains to the state."

A small pack scored a direct hit on the side of his head. At that moment, the door opened and a harsh voice cracked, "On your feet!"

Jay realized that without a doubt, he was facing Sergeant Grant. The sandy moustache quivered beneath the shiny peak of the dress cap as Grant started to erupt.

"What are you on, Kerr? Why aren't you in class?"

"I came up for a notebook I'd forgotten," Dick said brazenly.

"Well join the class and don't let me catch you malingering again."

Dick adjusted his beret at a rakish angle, picked up a notebook and departed.

Grant examined Jay coldly. "Not much doubt about who you are, is there? You're Williams, the man who was sent to Catterick yesterday morning to pick up a Land-Rover for the colonel. What happened to you?"

"It wasn't ready until this morning."

"Well, where is it now? Haven't you heard of reporting in when you finish a detail?"

"It's in the courtyard, Sergeant. I only came up to drop my things."

Grant cast up his eyes in horror. "God knows what sort of an army it is these days," he intoned piously, "But I'll have some changes around here if it kills me. Report to the orderly room with the vehicle's documents and then join your class."

He paused in the doorway and, with a disapproving

eye, surveyed the beds and the odds and ends draped around the room. "You get this room cleaned up as well," he said. "You might live like this where you come from, but it won't do here." With a final glare, he strutted away down the corridor.

Jay folded his greatcoat and hung it neatly behind the door. He shook his head and said softly, "I knew it was too good to last."

*

It was about nine o'clock when Jay and Dick entered the bar of The Tall Man. They beat a hasty retreat into the lounge at the sight of Sergeant Grant's burly figure leaning against the bar. His cropped head was inclined towards the landlord's daughter with whom he was enjoying a whispered conversation.

"They always say an old soldier is never short of a bit," Dick said in a dismal tone. "I wouldn't mind, but I've been after her for a fortnight and all she ever gave me was the air."

"She knows your intentions," Jay said. "Strictly dishonourable. Now the sergeant might get serious." He went to the serving hatch and came back with two beers.

"Cheers," Dick said and took a long swallow. "Life may get rough, but I'm damned if we'll let it get us down. Tell you what, we'll have a night in Rainford on Saturday. If we take the Jag we don't need to worry about last buses. As a matter of fact I just happen to know a rather nice little thing. Met her in a cinema yesterday. Now if she should have a friend anything like her . . . Well, believe me, we'll have a hell of a night."

Jay choked on his beer. "For god's sake, Dick, how on earth do you manage to meet them."

"Charm, old boy. Simple, manly charm. But how about it?"

Jay shook his head. "Sorry, Dick, I'm booked."

Dick grinned evilly and clapped him on the shoulder. "You old dog. Sneaked out and fixed yourself up, eh?"

"It isn't like that," Jay said. "She's only fifteen."

Dick laughed uproariously and then at the sight of Jay's face, stopped. "I say, you're not serious?"

Jay nodded. "It's a kid I met at a concert at Rainford Museum. She lives just outside Haxby so I gave her a lift home."

"And then what?"

"And then nothing. Listen, Dick, she's a really sweet kid. The concert was rotten and she simply suggested going to see Moura Lympany and the Hallé on Saturday. She can get tickets. Anyway, I like going to concerts. You know that."

Dick nodded several times, a look of fatherly understanding on his face. "I know, old boy, you just want to hear Moura Lympany playing the piano."

"Now look here," Jay began, but Dick cut him short by rising and going to the serving hatch.

He brought another two beers and a packet of cigarettes. He started to transfer the cigarettes into his case and said, "I know the ropes in this chase-the-girl game. I've been at it with some measure of success since I was fourteen. Perhaps that's not so good, but the point is I've met some funny ones and there's nothing funnier than a funny woman. Funny peculiar I mean. I've seen some good boys get themselves into one hell of a mess and . . ."

"Cut it, Dick. I get the message. It may interest you to know that I *have* been out with a girl or two in my time, even before I met you."

"You could probably count them on the fingers of one hand," Dick jeered. "Look, Jay, I knew you from a distance at Cambridge. I heard about you. I heard what the proffs thought. You hardly did anything except study and train for middle-distance races. How much time did you have for women in those days?"

"You've made your point. What it has to do with the situation on Saturday, I don't know."

"Everything. You've been way up in the top room of that ivory tower of yours for so long that the air down here is going to your head. If you want a girl, let *me* know. I have a list as long as your arm. Anything from the quantum theorem to twisting. They all have one thing in common. They know what life is all about and they don't throw a hysterical fit if you put a hand on their thigh."

"I'm taking her to a concert, not to bed." Jay swallowed some beer and then laughed shortly. "Come to think of it *she*'s taking me. I would hardly suppose she has intentions in the other direction."

"You never know with women," Dick said darkly.

"But she isn't a woman—she's only a child."

"Believe me, old boy : a woman is a woman from the day she's born. Anyway, let's have another drink and we can toast your future appearance in the *News of the World*."

Jay moved over to the piano and began to play an old pre-war Gershwin number. Dick followed with the drinks and leaned on top of the piano listening attentively.

"They don't write songs like that any more," he said as Jay finished. "I wonder why?"

Jay shrugged and started to play another. "People lost something in the War, I suppose."

Dick nodded and said, "Heard anything about the book?"

Jay smiled. "I knew there was something. There was a letter for me when I got back. Professor Dawes read the manuscript and he's sent it to a publisher with a strong recommendation."

Dick grinned delightedly. "Good man. You're on your way, I can see it all. The impact on the world of learning will be tremendous. No university library will be complete without it. Then the book clubs will take it up. You'll be rich and famous, a professor at twenty-nine."

"Sounds great," Jay said. "We'll wait and see what the publisher says."

The book was of more importance to him than he cared to admit. It had grown from a thesis prepared during his research fellowship and as he played, he thought about what Dick had said.

Exaggeration, perhaps, and yet there was some truth. The book could help to make up for his more obvious disadvantages. There might still be a chance for a lecturer's post in one of the universities. The idea was pleasing. It wouldn't be such a bad idea to spend his life getting paid for what he enjoyed doing.

From the other bar came the sudden clamour of a handbell announcing closing time. The two friends successfully passed out into the night without being seen by Grant. They got into the car and Dick said, "That used to be such a nice little pub."

"And the piano was good," Jay said.

"Never mind, old man. I'll find us another, piano and all."

"Just make sure it's outside Grant's walking range," Jay said as they moved away.

*

The following morning was the first of the new régime. The brassy hardness of a bugle awakened them in semi-darkness.

Dick sat on the edge of the bed, cursing as he pulled on fatigue uniform. "Where the hell did he find a bugler?" he demanded in aggrieved tones. "If I get near the bloke who admitted to playing one of those damned things, I'll throttle him."

A voice drifted up from the courtyard, harsh and raucous. "Let's have you, then!"

"Come on," Jay said. "No sense in being late first morning and looking for trouble."

As they hurried downstairs Dick said plaintively, "And I thought it was going to be so cushy for the next year."

After roll-call Grant took them for a brisk three-mile run. He constantly bullied and threatened, running up and down the column and cursing the stragglers.

They arrived back at the house at six forty-five and stood in a shuffling coughing mass, their breath a white mist on the morning air.

"Breakfast at seven," Grant shouted. "Seven-thirty to eight, clean your rooms. Eight o'clock, outside in best B.D. and boots for drill. Classes start nine-fifteen from now on."

Fifty-seven disconsolate men crowded into the mess hall airing their opinions of Grant loudly. As Jay attacked his porridge, Dick leaned over the table and said, "I've got a great idea. Let's transfer to the Service Corps."

Jay shook his head. "I have a feeling he's going to be with us for always like a faithful shaggy old dog."

"When he retires I only hope he applies for a commissionaire's job at the head office of John Kerr and Son Ltd. I'll make him run with the letters by hand instead of posting them."

The greatest blow was saved until the last. As they were going to classes, they saw a group of men clustered round a notice board. Dick pushed his way through and a second later, gave an outraged howl.

"What on earth is it?" Jay said.

"Guard duty," Dick said. "Would you believe it, the bastard's put me on stag on Saturday night. Damn and blast him. Now I'll miss my date and that popsy was a sure thing."

"Never mind," Jay said consolingly. "We've something to be thankful for. If we ask old Suveroff nicely, he'll teach us some Russian swear words. You'll be able to tell Grant to his face what you think of him and he won't know what you're talking about."

Dick brightened. "That's the best idea you've had yet. Let's get working on it."

*

Just before three on Saturday, Jay was preparing to go out when Dick wandered in. "Take the Jag," he said. "Much better. You won't have to worry about the last bus. It leaves at ten."

"That's decent of you, Dick. I'll get some petrol in the village."

"Don't worry about that. She's full now."

Jay took his best uniform from the cupboard and Dick said, "Surely you're not going in that?"

"You know the extent of my wardrobe," Jay said. "An old Harris tweed jacket and a pair of cord slacks. Hardly elegant enough, even for a schoolgirl."

"We'll soon fix that." Dick went to the cupboard. "It's a good thing we're about the same build." He considered several garments for a while, and then said, "Voila! We have here one genuine Glencarrick thorn-proof sports suit." He flung it on Jay's bed and produced a light check shirt, hand-woven tie and brown brogues. "How will that do."

"I can't, Dick. There must be fifty pounds worth there."

"Get dressed, you'll keep the lady waiting."

Ten minutes later Jay tried to see himself in the in-adequate mirror. "How do I look?"

"Like an advertisement for one of those manly after-shaves that make a man smell like the backwoods in Autumn," Dick assured him.

"Well, I'd better be off," Jay said. "I must be at that bus stop before the bus or she'll get on."

"Got enough money?"

"Oh, yes. Plenty. Thanks all the same, Dick."

"Think of me tonight. Walking my lonely beat at the main gate."

"Tell you what, I'll bring you a drop of something when I come back," Jay promised as he left.

*

It was a beautiful afternoon with a nip in the air and a yellow sun sparkled on the mellowing leaves. He only took ten minutes to reach the bus stop in the Jaguar.

He lit a cigarette and waited. He could see the roof

of her home over the tops of the trees and he watched the gateway for a sign of her.

He had looked away briefly and when he turned to the gate again, a girl was walking across the road. She hesitated for a moment and then came towards the car.

"Hello, Jay," she said. "This *is* a surprise. Is the car yours?"

"No," he said vaguely. "It belongs to a friend of mine."

He gazed at her in amazement. She was wearing an expensive and beautifully cut light tweed suit. Her slim legs were encased in nylons and on her feet were half-heeled shoes. She carried a handbag in one hand and tan gloves in the other.

"Well," she said helpfully after a long pause. "I managed to get the tickets."

"Oh, did you? Good!" he said, and then suddenly realizing, jumped out of the car.

"I'm sorry. Get in, won't you? It's just that you look . . . different."

"Well, you look very nice, I must say. That suit must have cost a lot."

"I'm afraid it comes from the same place as the car," he said and she laughed delightedly.

As he started to get in she said, "Could we have the top down? It's such a lovely day."

He quickly lowered the hood and then climbed into the car. As they moved away, he stole a sideways look at her. Her black hair was long—as a woman's hair should be—and there was the merest trace of lipstick on her mouth.

Her hair was blowing back from her face and her cheeks were red and glowing. He took another brief look at her and suddenly felt absurdly and completely happy.

Chapter Three

They were soon passing through the outskirts of Rainford. As they approached the centre of the town the traffic became heavier and before long, they were crawling along in a procession of vehicles almost nose to tail.

"I never realized it was like this on a Saturday," he said.

"People come in from the smaller towns. It's a big shopping centre," Caroline said. "After six o'clock it's much quieter."

They cruised around for twenty minutes looking for a parking place without success. "This is hopeless," she said at last. "I suppose the restaurants will be just as crowded."

"We'll have to find somewhere," Jay said. "I'm hungry."

She pondered for a moment and her face brightened. "I know. We'll go up to the park. There's a café in the museum. It should be quiet there and the meals are quite good."

He swung the car out of the main traffic stream into a side street and they drove out towards the suburbs again.

"There's another way into the park," she told him. "I'll show you where to turn off. A road goes down to the lakeside and comes out by the jetty."

He parked the car by the jetty and they walked up to the museum. It was a beautiful evening with a touch of purple in the sky and the acrid scent of woodsmoke in the air.

The café was almost empty and they took a table in a secluded corner against a window that gave a fine view of the lake below.

They had egg and chips and a pot of tea and Caroline devoured enormous quantities of brown bread and butter and four cream cakes. Jay watched her in amusement, realizing how much of the child there was in her. They didn't speak much during the meal, but afterwards, replete and content, they began to talk.

"This friend who owns the car—he must be very rich?" she said.

"His father is. It amounts to the same thing. Ever heard of Kerr's Beer?" She looked suitably impressed and he went on, "Dick Kerr and I share a room at Greystones. As a matter of fact he was at Cambridge when I was doing research, but we moved in different circles then."

"Did he get a degree?" she asked.

Jay smiled. "As Dick puts it, only just. But he'll be going into the business when he gets out of the army so it doesn't really matter."

"He must be a nice person," she said. "I mean to lend you the car and the suit."

"He only has one real enemy—himself. But that's another story. He's on guard duty tonight so he couldn't use the car himself. He insisted I wear the suit to do full honour to you. I must say I'm glad he did, considering the way you look yourself."

She coloured prettily. "I didn't want you to feel ashamed of me."

He could not think of anything to say in reply to that. He lit a cigarette and the silence continued for a while until she said, "Where do you come from, Jay?"

"It's hard to say. I was born in Jamaica. My mother died soon afterwards, my father when I was about two."

"How awful for you." There was a wealth of sympathy in her voice. "Who looked after you?"

"An aunt in London—my father's sister. He brought me over after my mother died. He got a job in London and we lived with her. After he died she kept me on."

"It must have been hard for you," Caroline said.

He shook his head. "Not really. She had a café in the Portobello Road. I never went short of much. She kept me at the local grammar school, made me work until I got to university."

"She must have been a remarkable woman."

He nodded. "She died last year. I never did get the chance to pay her back properly."

For a moment they sat in silence and then she said, "What about another cup of tea?"

35

He pushed his cup over. "What time does the concert start?"

"Six-thirty. We've plenty of time."

He lit another cigarette and said, "Anyway, what about you? I only know your name and what your house looks like from the outside. Any brothers or sisters?"

Her face clouded slightly. "I'm the only one. I live with my grandfather."

"I see," Jay said carefully. "Just the two of you?"

"There's Mrs Brown. She comes from Haxby every day and does the housekeeping."

He hesitated for a moment and then plunged on. "And your parents?"

"My father was an army officer. He was killed in Korea. My mother lives in London." She rolled breadcrumbs into little balls between her fingers as she talked. "I suppose you've heard of *Fashion and Taste*?"

"Who hasn't?"

"My mother's the editor. She's what they call a successful career woman." She kept her eyes down and traced intricate patterns on the tablecloth with a fork. "She sent me to three perfectly good boarding schools including one in Switzerland. She was asked to move me from one and I left the other two myself. I couldn't live with her in London and go to a day school because she's a busy woman. She finally sent me up here to live with my grandfather. I'm glad she did. He's a darling." She looked up into Jay's face, the blue eyes suddenly vacant and empty. "I'm afraid I don't like her very much. Does that sound awful?"

He could think of nothing to say, no word that might help. They sat quietly for a little while longer and then she smiled brightly. "I'm afraid I feel a bit sorry for myself at times."

"We all do," he said. "It's like crying in a way. It relieves a certain kind of strain." He glanced at his watch. "I think we'd better make a move."

They strolled down towards the lake and she held his arm tightly and said, "What a perfect evening. I can't wait to get to the concert." She gave a child-like skip, and swung heavily on his arm.

"Heh, don't mind me," Jay said, "But mind the suit for heavens' sake."

She was immediately contrite and began to use that oldest of feminine tricks. She asked him about his work and professed a deep interest in history. Jay knew what she was doing, but did not really mind. There was a freshness in her approach that appealed to him and she had a trick of cloaking a shrewd point with innocent words. He told her about his studies and tried to explain the fascination of historical research.

They reached the car and as he handed her in she said, "I love the way your eyes flash when I start asking awkward questions. I think you have a terrible temper."

"On occasions," he said and climbed in beside her.

"If I was your wife would you beat me?"

There was a glint in her eye and he started to laugh. "Very probably."

He drove up the hill from the lake very fast and turned into the main road. There was little traffic now and the evening air was warm and pleasant. They didn't exchange another word until he pulled up outside the Town Hall. She gave him the tickets and they joined the large crowd moving in.

The hall was packed with people at least fifteen minutes before the concert was due to commence. Jay bought a programme and they scanned it together until a burst of applause indicated the entrance of the conductor. There was a moment of complete stillness and then the audience were swept into the exciting opening bars of *Don Juan*.

Jay was completely carried away as usual. It was almost with a sense of shock that he noticed people rising from their seats around him and realized that it was an hour later and the interval. He smiled at Caroline. "Enjoy it?"

She nodded. "I can't wait for the Concerto. Rachmaninoff is my favourite."

He became aware that he was holding her hand, realized he must have done so unconsciously for quite some time. He unclasped gently and said, "Let's go for a coffee. We've got ten minutes."

She settled for an orange drink and he joined the queue. It took him several minutes to reach the refreshment counter and as he started to force his way back through the crowd, he saw she was engaged in conversation with an elderly woman.

He handed Caroline her drink and she said, "Jay, I'd like you to meet Miss Johnson. Miss Johnson, this is a friend of mine, Jay Williams."

Jay switched his coffee hurriedly from his right hand to his left and shook hands.

"Miss Johnson takes me for history at school," Caroline informed him.

"How interesting," he lied.

Miss Johnson gazed at him with a slightly quizzical expression and he suddenly felt uncomfortable as Caroline babbled on. In about three brief sentences she mentioned his degrees, his book and the fact that he was on the Russian course at Greystones.

He quickly cut in on the conversation and began to talk about history with Miss Johnson. She discussed the problems of keeping up her classes' interest and flatteringly asked his advice.

He soon realized that what she was really trying to find out was his exact relationship with Caroline. The question showed in her penetrating grey eyes, in the mocking twitch discernible on her mouth from time to time. He prayed for release and as he prayed, the warning bell sounded.

"Good-bye, Caroline," Miss Johnson said. She smiled at Jay and extended her hand. He clasped it automatically. "It's been nice meeting you. I hope you enjoy the rest of the programme."

He turned and saw that Caroline was laughing.

"Poor Miss Johnson," she said as they returned to their seats. "She must be dying for Monday morning to come to see if I look different."

"And what's that supposed to mean?" he demanded, but the opening bars of the Concerto effectively silenced any further conversation.

Later, they stood with the rest of the audience and wildly applauded the superb playing and then made their way to the main entrance. As they descended the steps, Jay caught a glimpse of Miss Johnson watching them from the pavement below.

"There's that damned woman again."

"Oh, let's forget her," Caroline said. "That glorious music. I'm still floating on a cloud. I've no time for little people."

Seated behind the wheel of the car again he said, "What now? It's only nine o'clock. That must be early even for you."

"I shall ignore the last comment!" she said, as she leaned back against the seat and looked up at the stars. She placed a finger on her mouth and appeared to ponder deeply. "I know, let's go to a dance. They don't close until midnight. We'll have plenty of time."

He started the car and they moved away. "I noticed a dance hall on the main road," he said. "We'll try there if you like."

He parked the car in a side street and they walked up to the gaudily-painted entrance. A red and white neon sign flashed on and off and from inside the swing doors came a sudden blast of music.

A flat-nosed individual in tarnished gold braid held open the door and they moved inside. A young couple were already at the paybox. They got their tickets and turned away. Jay moved forward and held out a banknote. A hand flicked between him and the paybox and picked it up.

"What's the trouble?" Jay said.

A smiling man in a dinner jacket was holding the note out to him. "No trouble, sir. I'm afraid we're full, that's all."

"But two people have just gone in," Caroline said.

"That's right, madam," the man told her blandly. "Pity you couldn't have been a few minutes sooner."

She opened her mouth to protest and Jay took her firmly by the arm and led her away. The commissionaire held the door open for them and they went down the steps and turned along the street.

They got into the Jaguar and as Jay took the ignition key from his pocket, she put a hand on his arm. "Does that happen very often?"

"All the time," he said calmly.

"And you stand for it?"

He shrugged. "After twenty-three years it doesn't mean a thing."

But as he drove rapidly out into the country, his hands were shaking and anger formed into a hard knot that threatened to choke him. After a while he stopped the car. He lit a cigarette and they sat in silence.

"It doesn't matter, Jay," she said out of the darkness. "People like that don't count."

"Don't they?" he said.

She took one of his hands, held it tightly. "No, they don't."

And then the anger dissolved and he grinned. "It is a long time since I last let a thing like that bother me."

He switched on the engine, swung the car into a side road and put on speed.

"Where are we going?" she asked.

"A place Dick Kerr and I discovered one night. A pull-up café for truck drivers. Quite a lot of people seem to drop in for a late night meal. The food's pretty good. I think you'll like it."

A red glow in the sky beyond the dark mass of a farmhouse indicated their destination. He parked the car amongst a varied assortment of vehicles and they walked across the cinders to the café. They entered a large, brightly-lit dining-room.

"Hungry?" he said.

"Well, I *could* eat something," she replied, slightly shamefaced.

He steered her through the crowded dining-room into a smaller side room that was empty. Jay went to a hatch that opened into the kitchen and ordered bacon sandwiches and tea.

The entire length of one wall was lined with fruit machines and pin-tables and Caroline busily hunted in her handbag for pennies. Jay slipped into the other room and changed a half-crown at the paydesk. He poured a stream of pennies into her handbag.

She looked up quickly. "Jay, you darling."

He soon lost the few coppers he had kept for his own use. Occasional groans indicated the varying fortunes of Caroline. He turned from the machine which had taken his last penny and discovered her furiously searching her handbag again.

"I haven't any left," she wailed.

"I gave you two shilling's worth."

"Well, I've got a ten shilling note. I'll get it changed."

He pushed her down into a chair. "Nothing doing. You can play these things all night and end up losing your shirt."

She giggled. "I don't wear one." At that moment the sandwiches and tea arrived.

When they had finished, he glanced at his watch and saw that it was just after ten. "When do you have to be in?"

"Grandfather doesn't mind. He keeps funny hours himself."

"Eleven o'clock will be plenty late enough."

"Ridiculous!" she said indignantly. "I don't go to bed at that time on a Saturday when I stay in. Besides, it's Sunday tomorrow. Don't have to get up until church time. I can go to late Mass."

He crossed to a large, chrome and glass juke box that stood against the opposite wall, inserted a coin and selected a record. The music swelled out and he walked back to her.

"You wanted to go to a dance. We'll have one on our own."

She smiled up at him and moved lightly into his arms. They danced well together. She moved gracefully and surely, following his steps around the floor.

"Where did you learn to dance?" he asked.

"School. The girls dance with each other. It's a bit difficult if you're used to being the man and leading. I'm lucky. I always play the girl."

As the record came to an end, Jay turned to put another coin in the juke box and saw with some surprise, that several other couples had joined them. Someone else selected a record and they started to dance again.

Her cheek rested against his shoulder. He dropped his head a little and his lips touched her dark hair. He became aware of a compelling fragrance and swiftly raised his head and eased away. He was suddenly acutely conscious of the young body so firmly pressed against his. When the record finished, he suggested going home.

He drove slowly in the direction of Haxby and Caroline rested her head against his shoulder and sighed. "I don't want to go home yet."

They topped a slight rise and she moved away from him sharply and cried, "Stop the car, Jay! Stop the car!" He hurriedly slowed down and she said, "It's like a great big jewel box in the Arabian Nights."

Below them was spread the great sprawling mass of the city, thousands of lights glowing like cigarette ends through the darkness.

"It's certainly quite a sight," he said.

"It makes a perfect ending to the evening."

"Have you enjoyed it so much?"

"Enjoyed it? If only you realized." There was a sad intensity in her voice and he tried to see her expression in the dim light thrown up from the dashboard. She looked out over the lights of the city. "When I get married I'm going to have five children—at least five. And I shan't leave them for a minute—not ever."

For a moment he was going to reach out to her through the darkness. To tell her that he also had been lonely and that he understood. Instead, he said, "I'd better get you home," and he started the engine and drove away.

Chapter Four

He turned in through the gates at Greystones shortly after eleven. An arc light had been fitted to one gate post to illuminate the area. Dick was leaning nonchalently against the new sentry box reading a magazine.

He glanced up and said, "Hello, old man. Halt, who goes there!"

"Without a rifle?" Jay said.

"It's in the box. Don't want to get it rusty in this damp night air. Did you remember my drink?"

Jay shook his head. "To tell you the truth, I haven't been near a pub all night."

"Indeed?" Dick peered into the car. "I hope you haven't messed my new seat covers up."

"Don't you ever think of anything else?" Jay said. "If you must know, I never touched her."

"Good show, old man. You'll feel a lot healthier for it in the morning. Anyway. I'll settle for a smoke. I've run out." He opened the door and climbed into the car.

"What about Grant?" Jay said as they lit cigarettes.

"Went out at ten. Wanted to get to The Tall Man

before closing, I suppose. From the look in his eye I should say we'll be lucky to see him for breakfast—on Monday."

At that moment the figure of the relief guard emerged from the darkness. "Where the hell have you been?" Dick said. "Eleven o'clock we should have changed." He tapped Jay on the arm. "Let's go."

Jay ran the car round to the courtyard and they entered the kitchen door and walked through to the cloakroom in the entrance hall which had now been converted into a guard room.

In the centre of the room there was an old fashioned stove with a soot-blackened pipe that reared up through the ceiling. There were three beds against the wall and from two of them came the rhythmic breathing of the other members of the guard.

Dick pulled off his webbing belt and beret and threw them on the unoccupied bed. "Have some cocoa. Guaranteed to keep you awake all night."

He picked up two tin mugs and gingerly poured a dark-brown liquid from the battered pot that bubbled steadily on top of the stove. They sat on stools and sipped the cocoa and smoked. "What kind of night did you have?"

"Not bad."

"You don't sound very enthusiastic. Any trouble?"

Jay helped himself to more cocoa. "Not trouble exactly." He brooded quietly for a moment. "You know how it is. I was on the look-out for people giving me the fish-eye all evening."

"My god," Dick said, "are you still on that tack? Poor little black boy. When are you going to start spitting right back in their faces?"

"It's more than that," Jay said. "She looks her age —that's the trouble."

"Did you enjoy her company?"

"I certainly did." Jay shook his head. "She's a funny little thing. A peculiar blend of innocence and maturity." He related the evening's events.

"I must say her mother sounds a pretty hard apple," Dick said. He offered him another cigarette and went on, "If you want my advice, cut it off now—and I mean now. If it goes any further things could get complicated."

"I promised to go for tea tomorrow," Jay said. "She wants me to meet her grandfather."

"Don't go. Just forget about it."

Jay shook his head. "I can't do it like that. There's more to this than you appreciate. She's desperately lonely with very few friends. I should imagine she finds little in common with girls of her own age. She's pretty advanced. In fact she's a remarkable girl altogether."

Dick seemed amused. "You know, one would think you were seriously interested in the girl."

"It's Caroline who seems to be interested in me," Jay said. "My trouble is finding the right way to end the relationship before it goes too far."

"Telephone her. Tell her you're going to be busy in the near future. If she's as intelligent as you say, she should be able to take a hint."

"I've got it," Jay said. "She's going to Mass in the morning."

"And how exactly is that supposed to help?"

"We can wait outside and I can tell her something came up. Explain it nicely away. Promise to telephone her when I'm free and forget about it."

"What's all this 'we' business? What do you need me along for?"

"Moral support. She's so damned sweet I mightn't have the courage to lie to her if I'm on my own. You're the biggest rogue I know. You should be able to back me up admirably."

Dick laughed. "Thanks for the compliment. Actually, I wouldn't mind coming along. I'd very much like to see the remarkable Miss Grey."

Jay stood up and yawned. "I'll see you in the morning. If we get down there for eleven we should be in plenty of time to meet her."

"Pleasant dreams, old man," Dick said. "I'll wake you up around seven with a nice cup of tea."

"You do and you'll go out of the window and it's a long way down to the courtyard," Jay said with a grin as he left.

*

It was another fine morning as they drove down to the little church and parked outside. Jay was feeling seedy. He had not slept well and it didn't make him feel any brighter to see that Dick was as fresh and clear-eyed as if he had had twelve hours' sound sleep. They sat

49

in the car and talked rather aimlessly until the people began to come out of the church. He scanned the crowd attentively and then he saw her.

"There she is."

Dick straightened abruptly. "You don't mean the girl in the little red straw hat?"

"I do indeed," Jay said and called to her.

"But she's exquisite," Dick whispered.

Caroline swung gaily across to the car, a smile of pleasure on her face. "What a nice surprise."

"Hello, Caroline," he said and lapsed into silence.

She looked lovely. She was wearing a belted fawn coat and the red straw hat that Dick had remarked upon. Her eyes sparkled crystal clear and blue and there was a deep crimson flush on her cheeks. She looked clean and fresh and incredibly alive.

Dick coughed pointedly and Jay gathered his scattered wits. "Caroline, this is Dick Kerr."

Dick opened the car door and got out. "Jay's told me a lot about you. I may say he failed to do you justice."

She smiled warmly and glanced at Jay who was sitting rather morosely in the car. "What nice compliments he gives, Jay."

Jay felt unaccountably annoyed. "He's an expert at pleasing women if that's what you mean."

"If you're going home, we'll give you a lift," Dick cut in smoothly. "No trouble."

He handed her in and climbed behind the wheel. The atmosphere was distinctly cool as they drove away and Jay lit a cigarette, rather obviously omitting to give Dick one.

Caroline turned to him. "Were you waiting to see me?"

Jay seemed to have forgotten everything he had meant to say and Dick said quickly, "We were waiting for the pub to open. Jay remembered you were going to church this morning and I said I'd like to meet you."

They were already approaching her home and she told Dick to drop her off at the gate.

"Thanks for the lift," she said. "Don't be late this evening, Jay. Five o'clock."

He managed a smile. "I'll be there."

A thought seemed to strike her and she said to Dick, "Would you like to come too?"

He shook his head regretfully. "Unfortunately I have already fixed something else."

She grinned mischievously. "I hope you have a nice time and that she does as well."

He smiled warmly and swung the car in a tight circle until they faced towards Haxby. "I'd willingly do a swop, Caroline. See you again and I'll take you up on that invitation."

He took the Jaguar away in a mighty burst of speed and a skidding of wheels.

"You bloody show-off," Jay said. "What are you trying to do? Make her think you're Stirling Moss?"

Dick laughed jeeringly. "You're jealous, that's what's the matter with you, and I don't blame you."

"If that's your usual line, I don't know how you get away with it," Jay said. "And what about tonight? You were a lot of help, I must say. Do you realize I'll have to go now?"

"And why not?" Dick said, apparently forgetting all his previous remarks. "I'd go myself if I had the chance. She's a lovely, delightful girl, a special kind of girl. Anyway, what does her age matter? Juliette was only thirteen and girls got married at twelve in medieval times."

Jay shook his head and sighed. "You can change your point of view more quickly than a politician."

Dick swung the car into the yard of The Tall Man. "I've no time for a fellow who can't change his mind when the facts are presented to him in a different light," he said as they got out. "Caroline is in a very different light as far as I'm concerned."

Jay caught him by the arm and turned him round. "Dick, I love you like a brother, but so help me. If you get any of your usual ideas, I'll break every bone in your body."

For a moment, the smile on Dick's face froze and then he laughed. "Come off it, old man. I'm not as bad as all that." He clapped Jay on the shoulder and they went into the bar.

*

It was about four-thirty when they left Greystones. Dick was driving into Rainford and had offered to drop Jay off. He pulled up outside Caroline's house and grinned. "Have fun, old man. You'll be able to get back on your own, won't you? I have an idea I mightn't be home until breakfast." There was a grinding of gears and in a second he was nothing but a fast-dwindling noise in the distance.

Jay entered the gates and walked along the drive. At the far end of the garden, a large white-haired man worked among some plants. He stood up to stretch and looked across at Jay and bent to his work again with no sign of welcome.

Jay decided it would be just like Caroline to issue an invitation without first consulting her grandfather. The house was in full view now. It was pleasant and old and he judged it to have about ten rooms. Steps led to the front door which was not in a central position, for most of the length of the front of the house was taken up by a terrace enclosed in glass.

There was a deep barking and a Labrador skidded round the corner and charged at him. Jay stood perfectly still and the dog stopped dead, then advanced slowly and sniffed at his feet.

Caroline's clear voice called, "Digby! Come here at once." The Labrador wheeled and raced back at once. When Jay reached the steps she was standing at the top patting the dog's ears.

"Don't scold him," Jay said. "A dog's not much good if he licks a stranger's hand the first time he sees him."

"He wouldn't have bitten you anyway." She smiled.

"I'm glad you could come. We'll have tea as soon as grandfather comes in."

A deep voice rolled across the garden. "Has your friend arrived, Caroline? I'll be in directly."

"All right, grandfather." She held out her hand. "Come on in. You can help me with the tea things. I thought we'd have it on the terrace while there's still a little sun left."

He took her hand and followed her in. "I saw your grandfather as I came up the drive. He didn't say hello, so I was wondering . . ."

"Didn't I tell you?" She interrupted. "He's blind."

"I see," Jay said blankly.

"He's so good at getting about that I just never think about it."

"Have you told him about me?"

"That you're a Jamaican?" She nodded. "Why?"

"I wouldn't like to think I was here under false pretences, that's all."

"You're here because I want you here," she said. "Now come and help me get ready."

They had barely finished arranging the food on a small table on the terrace when a deep, mellowed voice sounded from the doorway. "I hope I haven't kept you waiting. I had to wash my hands."

He was one of the largest men Jay had ever seen. He must have been six-feet-four or five with a great breadth of shoulder. His hair was a snow-white mane swept back behind his ears and he wore an open-necked shirt and corduroy jacket.

He appeared to look directly at Jay and smiled and said, "How do you do, Mr Williams. I'm Jonathan Grey, Caroline's grandfather."

Jay smiled into the cloudy, opalescent eyes and shook hands.

The old man eased his great body into a wicker chair and said, "Sit down, my boy. I don't know if you're hungry, but I certainly am. Luckily, we eat a good Yorkshire tea here. Somewhat different from the southern variety."

Caroline tried in vain to smother a sudden spurt of laughter as she handed round the cups.

"And what might be amusing you, young lady?" he inquired mildly.

"It's just that I once told Jay you would call him your boy and you just have."

"One of the privileges of age, my dear."

"I must say this conversation is beyond me," Jay said. "The whole thing seems to be getting involved!"

"The tortuous paths of a woman's mind are beyond the understanding of mere men," the old man told him solemnly.

"Oh, damn you both!" Caroline said. "It was bad enough having grandfather on at me all the time. Now I've got you as well, Jay." She lifted the silver teapot. "More, anyone?"

Jay handed her his cup, a slight smile fixed on his face. "And now I've got you as well, Jay." Could it be a permanent relationship that she had in mind, then? He realized suddenly that from the very first, it must have been more than a casual affair to her. She must have felt some deep attraction—not just a physical one. He had come to know her so well that he was sure on that point.

No, she had spoken to him for a few seconds in the museum and he now knew that she must have followed him down to the lake. He swallowed his tea, wishing fervently that he had never come here. Something told him he was walking into a situation full of unknown pain and anguish.

Jonathan Grey was addressing him and he came out of his reverie with a start. "I'm sorry, sir. I didn't quite catch what you were saying."

"That's all right, Mr Williams, I . . ."

"Call me Jay, sir, please."

"Very well." The old man groped on a side table. His hand found a box of carved teak and he offered it. "Cheroots. I always smoke 'em. Bad habit from my wasted youth."

Jay took one of the long oily sticks and placed it between his teeth. He gave the old man a light.

Caroline began to pile things on to the trolley. "I'll tidy up the kitchen and wash the dishes. Don't want to leave a mess for Mrs Brown to come back to in the morning."

Jay jumped up at once. "You can't do them all yourself. I'll come and dry for you."

"Stay and talk to grandfather. You'll only get in the way." She vanished into the interior of the house pushing the trolley in front of her.

Jay settled back in his chair again. The cheroot was proving to be not half as bad as he had expected. The old man leaned towards him and said in a conspiratorial manner, "Now we can have a drink. The doctor told me to cut it down a little and Caroline interprets that to mean none at all. There's a bottle behind the books on the third shelf on your left as you enter the drawing-room. The glasses are in the cabinet; you can't miss them."

Jay grinned and followed instructions. He was back in a couple of seconds. "Three fingers for me," the old man said. "Better put the bottle back where you found it before she returns."

Jay poured himself a short one and went and hid the bottle again. The old man leaned back with a sigh of contentment. "In a way, I enjoy it more now that my supply is cut down. Funny, isn't it?" Jay murmured something and Jonathan Grey continued. "Caroline tells me you're a historian? That you're not a professional soldier?"

Jay explained his position. He felt relaxed and at ease, at peace with the world. Greystones and Grant and the struggles of his early years suddenly seemed of little consequence. He could speak of them to this man easily and without bitterness.

The evening was drawing in and night was close at hand. A small wind began to rustle through the branches of the trees outside and somewhere, a tendril of loose ivy tapped against a window.

He became aware that it was almost dark and that

he must have been talking for some considerable time. He stretched forward and looked at his host. He could see him now as a vague mass against the evening sky that glowed through the glass wall behind him.

"I must have droned on for a long time."

Jonathan Grey stirred in his chair. "It was interesting, Jay *and* informative, I feel that I now know a little about Jay Williams—the real Jay Williams, I mean."

"Caroline's taking her time, isn't she?" Jay said.

"She'll be back shortly," the old man said casually.

And then Jay realized the truth. Caroline refusing his offer of help was a part of it. He had been deliberately left alone with the old man. That was why he had been encouraged to talk about himself so freely.

He was angry, but in some strange way, amused at the same time. He leaned forward. "Will I pass, Mr Grey? Will I make a fit companion for your granddaughter?"

The old man laughed softly. "I was waiting for you to say that. You had me worried. I began to think that perhaps you weren't as perspicacious as I'd hoped. But I'm sure you'll forgive me. Caroline is very dear to me. She is more like me than she is like her mother, both in her mind and in her temperament. She arrives home bursting with news of a friend she has made— a man friend. Naturally, I was interested. You should be flattered, by the way. You're the first. To be honest, I expected nothing less in you than I have found. I have great faith in her judgement."

"Then you've no objection to Caroline and I continuing our friendship? It doesn't worry you that she should pick on an older man?"

"I don't see why it should. She's an unusual girl and she makes few friends. When she does, it's very certain indeed. And her mind operates on an intellectual level which I should say approaches your own. I'm sure you'll agree that's very important indeed."

Jay hesitated and then said slowly. "I think she finds me attractive—as a man, I mean."

"Which at least proves she's a normal, healthy young woman. Do you intend to take advantage of that?"

"I hope not," Jay said, "I like her too much."

"Then I can see no further objections. I'm a great believer in people sorting these little problems out for themselves. It's all a part of growing up, after all."

Jay got to his feet and paced along the terrace. "But it's not really as simple as that, is it? People will talk. Their minds can soil the most innocent affair."

"People?" said Jonathan Grey serenely. "What have men like you and I to do with people? Of course they'll talk. The fact that you're coloured will make things worse, I've no doubt. Must you deny yourselves the content of a happy relationship because of the attitude of the small-minded?"

Jay spread his hands and then dropped them to his sides. "I don't know. I'll have to think about it."

"Have you two talked enough?" Caroline had entered soundlessly in the dark.

"We've had a nice chat, Jay and I," her grandfather said. "It's getting chilly out here now. Let's move into the lounge."

"I've put the fire on," she said and took the old man's arm. They left the terrace, Jay walking behind.

A pleasant fire burned in a fine old Adam grate and the flames danced in the shiny surface of a grand piano that stood against the wall. Jay lifted the lid and played a few chords. "Does anybody mind?"

Jonathan Grey was settled in a wing-back chair by the fire and Caroline came over and lifted the top of the piano. "I didn't know you could play?"

"I get by," he told her, and slipped into an old Roger's and Hart number. Nostalgic and wistful. A hint of a summer that had gone.

He passed easily from one number into another. He was playing half-unconsciously, all the time searching for an answer to the problem of his relationship with Caroline. But it seemed hopeless. For all the old man's broad-mindedness it could lead nowhere. Nothing could come of it.

He stopped playing and glanced at his watch. It was almost eleven. "I think I should make a move."

"Oh, Jay," Caroline said reproachfully. "I was enjoying it so much."

"We'll see some more of you I hope," her grandfather said.

"Of course, sir. I hope you'll excuse me though. Reveille is at six and I have a hard day ahead."

"I'd forgotten there was such a time." The old man

half-raised a hand and Jay walked to the front door with Caroline.

They stood at the top of the steps and she shivered. "It's cold, but it shouldn't take you long to walk."

"I'll be all right. Thanks for everything. "He felt awkward, unsure of himself.

"When will we see you again, Jay?"

"I won't know what the week's training programme is until the morning."

"Give me a ring tomorrow night and let me know."

It was what he had hoped she would say. "Yes, that's the best thing. I'll say good night, then."

He walked down the drive, moving into the darkness until she was only a dim shape. There was a moment's silence and she said in a different voice, "Jay, you will telephone, won't you?"

"Good-bye, Caroline," he called and hurried into the protecting night.

Chapter Five

He walked rapidly along the main road towards
Haxby. After a while he slowed down to light a cigarette. He felt restless and keyed-up inside and he wondered if Caroline had sensed anything.

It was a quiet night, the only sound a dog barking
five fields away. He stood listening for a moment and
then a bank of cloud rolled away from the moon and
the countryside was bathed in a hard, white light. The
night sky was incredibly beautiful with stars strung
away to the horizon where the moors lifted to meet
them.

He looked at it all for several minutes and wondered
why everything was not as simple and uncomplicated
as an autumn night. You only had to stand and look
at it and it cost nothing but a little time and it gave
you so much.

He continued towards Haxby, walking through
quiet, deserted little streets that stirred uneasily in
their sleep as the clatter of his footsteps disturbed them,
and quietened again as he passed.

He had barely left the houses behind, when he heard
a sound approaching rapidly from the distance. He

stood at the side of the road and waited. He could see the headlights of a car coming very fast and the roar of the engine deepened as it started to pull up the slight gradient out of the village. A headlight picked him from the darkness and the car shuddered to a halt.

"Jump in, old man," Dick called. The car was moving again before Jay had even shut the door. "How did it go?"

"I don't know. Hard to say," Jay told him. "I thought you were spending the night out?"

"Fell through, old man. Damned woman didn't turn up. I went to this pub where they all meet and . . ."

"Just a minute," Jay said. "I thought you met this girl in a cinema?"

"This is a different one, old man. She's mixed-up with some group theatre effort. Amateurs and semi-pro's—very much so, from the looks of some of the girls. Anyway, I met this girl some time ago and arranged to see her at this pub where all the actors meet. She didn't come, but I got talking to another one from the same group theatre. Tina, her name is. A bit of all right, believe me."

"I'm sorry," Jay said. "I'm afraid I've completely lost count. I don't know who is who any more. I wish you'd stick to a girl for a couple of weeks. It would give my brain a rest."

"She had to be in at ten-thirty," Dick told him, ignoring the remark.

"That must have been a shock."

"Oh, I don't know. She's got something extra. I'm taking her out on Tuesday."

Jay pulled up his collar against the cold airstream and wondered about Dick. Eternally searching, always being disappointed. A happy lecher who had known many women and yet still believed in them. They crashed from their pedestals with clockwork regularity and he blithely put another up and hoped again.

When they reached the house they mounted the back stairs quietly and Jay hung his jacket behind the door and lay on the bed without undressing.

Dick produced a half bottle of whisky and poured a generous measure into two tin cups. They lay there in the dark, drinking and smoking.

Presently, Dick said, "Come on, Jay. Out with it. What happened?"

Jay began to talk, slowly and carefully, thinking about it all as he did so. He told Dick about Jonathan Grey and of their talk and how Grey didn't see anything wrong in the whole affair.

"You should be pleased about that," Dick said. "Your precious conscience is clear now. No one can say you're meeting the girl on the sly or anything like that."

"But I'm not going to see her any more," Jay said. "I've decided quite definitely. I'd only end up by liking her too much and where would that get me? All my life I've tried to do the sensible thing."

Dick's voice came drowsily from the other side of the room. "For whom? Yourself? Think of her a little.

In any case, if you never see her again, you may end up regretting it for the rest of your life."

Jay lit another cigarette and lay quietly thinking until he'd smoked it. There were pictures in the dark. Caroline laughing. Caroline tender and gay. Nothing but Caroline.

He stirred and said, "But if I do go on seeing her, what happens?" There was no answer. From the other side of the room came the sound of heavy breathing and he pulled a blanket over his shoulder, turned his face to the wall and tried to sleep.

*

The following day was noteworthy because Grant gave his first lesson in unarmed combat. It was just before tea-time on a rather chilly afternoon and the men stood in fatigue uniform and rubbers in the field at the back of the house and tried to look interested. Grant started by showing them some simple arm-locks and paired them off to try them on each other.

He constantly interrupted by demonstrating to various unfortunates how it should be done. Soon there were black looks and bruised arms as he passed among them.

Dick and Jay were taking it easy with each other and Grant stopped to watch them. "You pansies will never learn," he said disgustedly. "What happens if you ever have to face a man with a gun when you haven't one?"

Nobody volunteered a reply and Grant, who was

stripped to the waist, pointed to a puckered scar over his left breast and said, with simple pride. "That was made by a bullet. I killed the man who did it with my bare hands before I collapsed."

There was a murmur from the men and someone said audibly from the rear, "Oh, Sergeant," in lisping tones.

Grant's face purpled and he snarled, "All right, you humourists. I'll show you."

He turned to Dick. "Right, Kerr. Try and hit me." Dick looked unwilling. "Try and hit me on the jaw. That's an order." Dick swung inexpertly. Grant caught his wrist and threw him over his shoulder with needless brutality. Dick picked himself up, white and shaken and Grant said, "You next, Williams."

Jay moved in front of him. "This is what you do if a man is stupid enough to let you get close," Grant said and kicked him sharply under the left knee-cap. Jay, surprised by the sudden pain, doubled over. Grant raised a knee into his face and swung his fist down into the back of the unprotected neck.

Jay scrambled to his feet, blood oozing from his nose. "You can thank your lucky stars I was wearing rubbers," Grant said. "You'd have been crippled and out for the count if I'd had my boots on."

The class filed into the house to wash-up before tea, Jay and Dick hobbling along at the rear. "Why don't we wait for him one night?" Dick said. "Just the two of us. Nobody would ever know. We could give him the old one-two in a couple of seconds and then clear off."

Jay shook his head as he led the way into the wash-room. "He'd probably give us both a hiding and then where would we be?"

Dick sluiced water over his head and groped for a towel. "Sunny Colchester at War Office expense. You're right, I suppose."

Jay gingerly touched the tip of his nose and winced. "All the same, if he keeps on handing out this sort of treatment, he'll get it from somebody one of these dark nights. You can bank on that."

Dick went to look at orders and Jay was in the room pulling on his shirt when he came in. "Hard lines, old man. He's got you down for a guard on Thursday."

Jay shrugged. "It had to come. All the same, I wish they'd transfer him to the Foreign Legion. He'd fit in there much better, I'm sure."

*

They went for a drink that night, to a new pub Dick had discovered a couple of miles away down a narrow country lane. He had kept his promise and the piano was a good one. They passed a congenial evening and for once, Dick made no mention of the opposite sex.

On Tuesday night, he had a date with his new girl friend and Jay spent a quiet evening catching up on his Russian vocabulary. When Dick came in shortly after eleven, he talked about the girl quite a lot and announced that he was seeing her again the next night.

Jay decided she must be an improvement on the others. "At least you're in bed at a decent hour for a change."

"She's going to reform me, old man. She's begun to work already with a subtle alchemy. This is not the old Dick Kerr you see before you, but a clean, pure, all-British boy."

"For at least another week," Jay said sourly, putting out the light.

"What you need is the love of a good woman, my lad." Dick's voice mocked him from the darkness. "I could make a suggestion."

"Good night, Dick," Jay said with finality and pulled the blankets over his head.

*

The following evening after Dick had left, he followed the same pattern. He sat over his books from six till nine and finally stopped when his eyes began to hurt.

He decided to walk down to The Tall Man. The trouble was that he and Dick had kept to themselves too much. Now that he was on his own, he found that he hardly knew anyone else. His comrades were only names that were shouted harshly at morning roll call or in a guttural Russian accent by Mr Suveroff in class.

He stood at the bar and had a beer that he didn't really want. Someone was thumping away at a piano in the lounge and an enthusiastic audience was singing loudly.

There was a sudden flurry of movement and half-a-dozen of the boys squeezed through the locals and lined up at the bar. One or two of them nodded to Jay and passed a casual word. He felt completely alone, isolated from the crowd and their voices faded into a tremendous, meaningless murmur in the background. He swallowed the rest of his beer and left.

Just outside the pub there was a telephone box. He stood looking at it for several moments and then slowly walked past it and started back to Greystones. As he approached the edge of the village, he came to another public telephone. Every circumstance seemed to conspire against him, determined to make him do what he knew in his heart would be a great mistake.

He scrambled over the stone wall at the side of the road and cut across the parkland to Greystones. He wondered if Caroline still expected to hear from him? She was no fool—she was anything but a fool. He tried to recall the particular tone in which she had called out to him as he had left her on Sunday night.

She must have suspected then. She was proud, he was certain of that. Her pride would prevent her from approaching him again. There was a limit beyond which a woman was unable to go. That in itself was some protection for a man.

*

Dick announced next morning that he was to see the beautiful Tina again that night. "You're getting into a rut, aren't you?" Jay said.

"An enjoyable one, old man. Believe it or not, I'm

spending a quiet evening watching television. Most relaxing. You should try it."

"What's the attraction?" Jay enquired. "The fact that the room's in darkness?"

"Have a little faith in your old pal. I'm reformed, I tell you."

At breakfast, he asked Jay if he had arranged which turn he would be on with the other members of the night guard.

He had not bothered. "I'll take the luck of the draw," he said. "I do not care a hang when I go on as long as I get the damned thing over with."

*

When Jay went on guard that night, it had started to rain heavily. They had drawn lots and he had picked the first turn. He was sheltering in the sentry box shortly after seven when Dick passed through the gates.

"I never thought you'd be lucky enough to get the first turn," he shouted from the car. "That means you won't be on again until one a.m."

"You know that as well as I do," Jay said. "Why all the fuss?"

"It's just that I'll be in by eleven, so I'll miss you. Have fun." He slid away into the curtain of rain leaving Jay to pass two boring hours.

When he came off duty at nine he went straight to bed and was awakened shortly before one for his second turn. He sat on the edge of the bed and laced his boots. He felt rotten and there was a foul taste in his mouth.

He tried to pour a cup of cocoa from the pot and found to his disgust that it was empty. He pulled on his greatcoat, slung his rifle over one shoulder and walked down to the sentry box smoking a cigarette.

At least Grant could not be everywhere for twenty-four hours a day. Although the guard duty was unpleasant, it was easy enough. The sentry he relieved vanished thankfully in the direction of the house and Jay took shelter from the heavy rain in the sentry box. It was unlikely that anyone of importance would pass through at that time in the morning. He leaned his rifle in the corner and opened his greatcoat to get at his cigarettes.

He paused suddenly and stood quite still. He could have sworn he had heard his name called. The rain was driving against the roof with a persistent drumming and it made a rushing hiss as it fell through the trees. He fumbled for his cigarettes again and then he heard the voice quite distinctly.

"Jay!" Someone called. He stepped out of the sentry box and saw a light approaching along the road. As it drew nearer, he realized it was someone pushing a bicycle. Before he heard her voice again, he knew it was Caroline.

He ran forward, took the bike from her and leaned it against the box. "What on earth are you doing?" he said, pulling her under cover from the rain.

"It's nice in here," she remarked irrelevantly. "If

71

they gave you some heating, it wouldn't be half bad."

He pulled off her head scarf and touched her hair. He ran his hands lightly over her. "You're soaking." He took a handkerchief from his pocket. "Dry your hair with this."

She obeyed meekly. When she had finished, he unknotted his khaki wool scarf and said, "Put this round your throat. It's not much, but it's the best I've got. I'm not exactly equipped for visitors."

She held a bag up in front of him. "The supplies got through, commander. I've got a thermos of hot coffee and some sandwiches."

"You'll get me shot if anyone comes," he said. "But the coffee would be welcome. There wasn't a damned thing to drink when I got up." She handed him the thermos and he swallowed gratefully.

"I'm the perfect specimen of all-sufficient woman," she said. "The trouble is I'm in danger of *not* being taken for granted."

He avoided the opening and parried her remark with a question. "How did you know I'd be on duty at this time?"

"Dick telephoned me last night. He said the mountain wouldn't go to Mohammed so Mohammed would have to go to the mountain. He thought you'd be on duty about ninish. He called tonight to tell me you were on the early turn but I couldn't bother you then because too many people would be passing in and out. He said he'd have to think of something else. I didn't tell him I intended visiting you on the graveyard shift. Even he mightn't have approved."

"You're damned right he wouldn't," Jay said. "What are you trying to do? Catch pneumonia?"

"You warned me against that the first time we met."

"Well, I'm warning you again. You should go straight home and get into a hot bath." He stared out at the rain lancing down through the yellow light thrown out by the arc lamp. "I'd love to see Sergeant Grant's face if he knew I was sheltering in his precious sentry box with a woman."

"At last you've admitted it," Caroline said. "It's taken you long enough. How are you sure now? Of course, it's only a small sentry box and we are squeezed together rather. Perhaps this is what they call being really intimate."

"Shut up!" he said. There was a breathless moment of complete stillness. "Don't let me ever hear you talking like that again."

He lit a cigarette and she said in a small voice. "Could I have one? I've smoked before."

He gave her a cigarette and held out a match for her in cupped hands. As she drew on the cigarette she coughed a little and said in rather a high-pitched voice, "Don't worry. I'm definitely not going to be sick," and then she burst into tears.

He held her close and she buried her face into his chest and sobbed uncontrollably. "Oh, Jay, why didn't you phone? You promised you would."

"It's all right, Caroline. It's all right now." He stroked her hair gently.

"I'm so lonely, Jay," she said, "And I liked you so much. More than anyone I've ever known. I thought you liked me."

"But I do," he said.

"Then why have you acted in the way you have?" Her sobs had quietened a little now. "I'm young and I may seem stupid at times. But all I know is that I liked you and I came down here feeling rotten about everything. If you want me to go, please tell me—now."

For a moment, he hesitated and then took the final, irrevocable step over the edge. "No, I don't want you to go," he said.

Her eyes widened perceptibly in the light and then she flung her arms about his neck and hugged him, too happy to speak. Little broken sobs still racked her slight body and he held her close in his arms for a long time until finally she was quiet.

"I'm cold," she murmured after a while.

He opened his greatcoat and pulled her inside so that they were both encased in its rough warmth. "How's that?"

"I could stay here all night."

"Nothing doing. You're going in a couple of minutes." If anything, the rain had increased in force during the past half hour. "I wish you didn't have to go in weather like this."

"A little more rain can't hurt. What time is it?"

He glanced at his watch. It was almost two. "Is there another cup of coffee left in that flask?"

As he was drinking it, she packed the bag again and said, "Jay, why didn't you phone as you promised?"

He blew rings of cigarette smoke out into the darkness and said quietly, "Because I liked you too much and I didn't want to see you get hurt. You know what goes on in the world. The Sunday papers are full of it. Most people have minds like cess pools whether they're willing to admit it or not. When they see a man with a young girl, they start talking. When he's coloured into the bargain . . ."

He shrugged and Caroline said, "Mrs Brown, our housekeeper, spoke to me on Monday when she came in. She'd seen me talking to you and Dick outside the church on Sunday. Apparently she was quite shocked."

"A friendship can be as innocent as you like and people will still talk," Jay said. "I suppose it's all bound up with the fact that no one really believes that a platonic friendship between a man and a woman is possible."

At that moment, the rain increased into a torrential downpour. "We can't have you going home in this," he said. "Desperate measures call for desperate remedies. I shan't be long."

He buttoned his greatcoat and ran out into the darkness. He was soon drenched and his heavy boots splashed in puddles hidden by the night until his trousers were soaked as far as his knees.

He ran all the way to the house and did not stop until he had reached the courtyard. He pulled open the door of the old stable that Dick used as a garage and fumbled for a match. He was in luck for Dick had left his ignition key in the car.

Jay got behind the wheel and released the brake. The car rolled down the sloping cobbled floor of the stable and the impetus was sufficient to keep it moving out of the yard and into the drive. He was by now a reasonable distance from the house and he turned on the ignition and moved into gear.

He pulled up opposite the sentry box and shouted, "Quickly, then. I'll have to make it snappy."

Caroline ran forward and clambered in and he accelerated at once. "Jay, you fool," she said in a worried tone. "What if someone misses you?"

He did not reply and took the car forward with a surge of power into the dark, rain-swept night. He roared through the village and a couple of minutes later, changed down and skidded into the entrance of her house.

As the car stopped, she jumped out into the rain. "Don't stop to talk," she said. "Get back at once."

"I'll ride round on your bike tomorrow evening," he called and accelerated down the drive.

The speedometer needle flickered towards ninety on the stretch between Haxby and Greystones. He felt a tremendous elation and at the same time, complete confidence in himself. He decided to take a chance and drove like a madman along the drive to the house and went straight into the stable still in top gear. A moment later he was running headlong through the rain towards the gate, splashing in the puddles and not caring.

He stood trembling in the sentry box and stripped away his sodden greatcoat. He lit a cigarette with shaking hands and slumped back against the wall.

Suddenly he began to laugh, quietly at first and then louder. The sound echoed flatly through the heavy rain.

Chapter Six

Jay came off guard at 7.30. Apart from the usual grittiness under his eyelids he felt wonderful. As he mounted the stairs to the room he decided that the only good thing about guard duty was coming off it, for he was a free man until lessons started at 9.15.

A shower and then a leisurely breakfast while the rest of the boys sweated it out on the drill parade would be very nice. He shook his blankets out of the window and was busy folding them when Dick came in.

"Morning, old man," he said brightly. "Sleep well?"

"Well enough," Jay said.

Dick pulled on his best uniform and sat on the edge of the bed to lace his boots. "It must have been a lousy guard stuck in the sentry box all the time. It's not so bad on a fine night. I went for a walk up the road."

"It was all right," Jay said casually. "As a matter of fact, I took the car and went for a drive. Good thing you left the key in."

Dick sat up abruptly. "What happened?"

"Caroline," Jay said simply.

"Oh, my God! What time did she come?"

Jay explained. When he had finished, Dick said, "And they call *me* crazy. What would have happened if Grant had decided to do a check? He did the other night and caught some poor bloke smoking. Got him fourteen days C.B." He stood up and stamped his feet hard to make his trousers fall properly over his gaiters. "One thing seems obvious. You aren't going to knock my block off for interfering."

"No, damn you!" Jay said.

The well-known voice floated up from the court-yard like a banshee wail. "I'd better go," Dick said. "Be a sport and fix my bed, old man," and he rushed from the room.

Jay listened to the shouted commands outside and then, with a feeling of complete well-being, went down to the mess hall for late breakfast.

*

Jay cycled to Caroline's house after tea and found her grandfather pottering about in the garden. He walked towards him and called out, "Hello there."

Jonathan Grey lifted his head. "So you changed your mind?"

"It was changed for me."

The old man smiled enigmatically. "She's in the kitchen. Don't let me keep you. I'll see you later."

Jay entered the front door and made his way to the rear of the house. A green baize door looked promising and he opened it. Caroline was standing at the sink washing crockery.

He closed the door quietly and said, "What's for tea?"

She swung round at once, a look of surprise on her face. "Jay! You're earlier than I expected."

"This time I insist on drying for you." He took off his tunic, rolled up his sleeves and picked up the tea towel. "Any plans for this evening?"

"You're going to do some work for a change," she said. "I promised Father Costello I'd be down at the hall tonight to give a hand with the decorations for the children's party on Saturday. You can come and do the heavy work."

"Thanks very much."

"He's looking forward to meeting you."

"Then I'd better be on my best behaviour."

*

They walked down to Haxby through the quiet evening and she tucked her hand into his arm. "You know, I've decided that a uniform suits you."

"Personally, I can't wait for the day I shall get out of it for good."

"Don't look at it that way. Everything has a purpose. Everything works out for the best. If you hadn't joined the army, you wouldn't have met me."

A warm smile crinkled his face. "That would definitely have been a great pity."

They were passing a draper's shop at that moment and were reflected perfectly in a large mirror.

"See what a handsome couple we make?" she said.

"You should see me on my good days," Jay replied and they were still laughing when they arrived at the church.

The hall stood at the rear, a single-storeyed brick building with a corrugated iron roof. On entering, they passed through a cloakroom into the hall itself. There was a murmur of conversation from a side room and Caroline led the way in.

Several young girls and boys were standing in a group talking to the priest. Caroline said, "Hello, Father. I hope we've not kept you waiting. I've brought you some muscle to make up for it."

Father Costello smiled affectionately at her and turned to Jay. He was short and stocky, with a shock of iron-grey hair falling over his forehead. He looked a very able man and smiled as he extended a hand.

"I'm happy to meet you."

Jay became aware of the stares of the youngsters and again he felt a faint disquiet, an unease that always seemed to strike at the heart of his relationship with Caroline.

"Well, Father," he said. "Where do we start?"

"I'll set the young ones to work and then the two of us can begin," Father Costello said.

He sent the girls to the Presbytery to help his housekeeper prepare the refreshments and gave some of the boys addresses in the village where chairs might be borrowed.

Caroline gave Jay a little smile. "See you later," she said and went out with the other girls.

For the moment, Jay and the priest were alone. Jay took out his cigarettes. "Mind if I smoke, father?"

"Indeed not. I'd like one myself if you can spare it."

They lit cigarettes and the priest said," It's decorations for us, Mr Williams. I'm afraid I'm not a great deal of use, but I can hand things up if you'll tack them into place. We've got some step-ladders here, but I've no head for heights."

Jay felt a sudden irritation at the use of his surname. In his mind, it made a distinction between the priest's familiar use of the young people's Christian names, including Caroline's as if he was stressing the fact that he and Jay were adults.

As he placed the step-ladders in position he said, "I wish you wouldn't call me Mr Williams, Father. It isn't my official title any more. Jay will do fine."

The priest smiled faintly and handed him one end of a coloured streamer and some drawing pins. "Caroline's a wonderful girl."

"The best," Jay said, pinning the streamer into place.

The priest stepped back to examine his handiwork. "Very nice, Jay. Very nice. Tell me, do you go to church?"

Jay shook his head and moved the ladder along the wall. "I stopped believing a long time ago, Father."

The priest handed up more decorations. "Might I ask why?"

"Because it doesn't work," Jay said. "Not for people like me."

The priest sighed. "We're not likely to see you at Mass in the near future then?"

Jay grinned. "If Caroline had her way, I'd probably be there every Sunday from now on."

"She mentioned you to me the other day. She gave me a very comprehensive account of your background. I would say she's in love with you." Father Costello said it very quietly and casually.

"Is there anything wrong in that?" Jay said. "How do you know I'm not in love with her?"

"She's only a child."

"Love has a rather whimsical habit of breaking out in a rash where it chooses, Father, like the measles. I don't think it takes age into account. In any case, I wish people wouldn't look at me as though I'm a dirty old man. I'm only twenty-three."

"My dear boy," the priest began, "You must look at this affair from the angle of what will turn out best for Caroline. The world condemns what it sees; seldom what exists under its nose if it's well enough concealed."

"In other words Caroline would be better choosing some young fool who happens to be of an age with her? Intellectual and mental requirements mustn't be taken into account?"

The priest looked pained. "I don't think that at all. I'm sure your relationship is innocent not only because of my knowledge of Caroline, but because I think you're a good man. The world is very unfair at times. As I've just said, it condemns things on their face value. There are people among my parishioners—good people—who will place one interpretation on a friend-ship between a fifteen-year-old girl and a man of your age."

"Shouldn't you qualify that, Father? Shouldn't it be a coloured man of my age?"

"Perhaps," Father Costello said.

"Then you've failed in your work."

"That isn't true. Say rather that we're all human being and carry within us many faults. I don't say that the gossip will be true or that such an outlook is a Christian one. I only wish to point out that it is the attitude people will have. It can only have one effect in the long run."

"If these are my fellow men then I cut myself off from them. As for their opinion," Jay snapped his fingers, "I don't give that for it. If people choose to invent what doesn't exist, then the fault is theirs."

Father Costello shook his head sadly. "You expect perfection in a world where there is none. We do the best we can, all of us."

He began to gather up the remaining pieces of coloured paper and paused for a moment looking down at the floor. "You are set on your course and I can't stop you. As for Caroline, if I attempted to turn her away from you, it would only cause her to lose confidence in me and I can't allow that to hap-pen."

A buzz of conversation signalled the arrival of the

boys with the chairs and trestle tables. Jay made a bad attempt at a smile and said, "Well, Father, now we've disposed of that, I'll give the boys a hand."

The priest nodded, turned abruptly and left the room.

*

It was after nine when they had finished. Caroline was delayed by some minor job until after the others had left and Jay idly picked out a tune on the battered piano.

He felt moody and disturbed and the words that the priest had spoken would not leave his mind. Why were people like that? Why did the average human being descend so easily to such a level?

"Sorry I kept you." Caroline walked across from the kitchen. "Some of the cakes didn't have the lettering on them."

"That's all right," he said. "You look tired. I'll take you home."

She smiled wanly. "There was such a lot to do and most of the girls couldn't stay very long. We had to work very hard to get it all ready."

They went out into the night and walked round to the front of the church. She turned to him, her face a white blur. "Do you mind if we go in for a moment?"

He took her arm. "Of course not."

She went ahead of him, dipped a knee and crossed herself and he slid into the seat beside her.

The light in the church was very dim and up at the

altar the candles flickered and the Holy Mother seemed to float out of the darkness bathed in a soft white light. The sweat sprang to his temples and then he sighed and relaxed, remembering that it was only an image.

Beside him rose the quiet murmur of Caroline's voice in prayer. The smell of the incense was overpowering and he felt giddy and light-headed. He stretched out a hand in the darkness and found the cold roughness of a pillar in front of him. It brought him back to reality quickly. Through the quiet, he heard a soft whisper as though a very small wind had crept through the church and he leaned forward, his forehead resting against the cool pillar.

There was a movement beside him and Caroline got up and went up to the altar. She lit a candle placed it in a holder and prayed for a while. Wher she returned, her face was shining with ecstasy.

They walked back slowly through the calm night. They said nothing, for there was nothing to say and Jay had never felt so close to anyone in his life.

When they reached the house, she moved ahead of him to open the front door. "Grandfather will be in the lounge. You go on in. I'll make some supper."

The light was out and the room looked comfortable in the red glow of the blazing fire. Jonathan Grey sat in the wing-back chair, a cheroot between his fingers, his face turned towards the hissing logs.

Jay slipped into the opposite chair. "What do you see there in the flames?"

The old man turned his head sharply. "Hello, Jay. Didn't hear you come in. How do you know I can see anything?"

"I don't believe a man like you sits like that with an empty mind. If you haven't always been blind, your own fire images must return in the dark."

Jonathan Grey chuckled softly. "How well you understand. Yes, I see fire images." His hand groped for the teak box. He held it out and Jay took a cheroot. "I see a ship heeling into the wind, her decks awash. I see a young man, strong as a bull, a fugitive from convention and respectability, hauling himself into the rigging, laughing into the wind and not caring. I can see him through forty adventurous years. Africa in the old days, China and India—several wars of varying size and importance." He chuckled again. "What a life I've led. What a damnably roguish life."

"Regret it?" Jay said.

"Never regretted a minute of it. Not a damned minute, mistakes and all. If I regretted the life I've led, that would mean I regretted living, wouldn't it? No, it's been wonderful."

"What about people?"

"They're all right on the whole. Take them as they come, I've always said. I never cut much ice with my relatives. They thought I was just a bloody adventurer. The only time they ever fell on my neck was when I got a Polar Medal from the old king. That made me respectable, but only temporarily."

"What was Caroline's father like?"

"Very much like me. He was my only son, you know. Caroline's dear mother, Margaret—she tried to hold him down, change him into what she wanted him to be."

"What happened?"

"In the end she only succeeded in driving him away. The Korean War broke out and he volunteered for active service again. He was killed in a patrol action near the Yalu River. In a queer sort of way, Margaret has blamed me ever since because I handed down my wildness to him. And that was the one flaw in him as far as she was concerned. She's grown into a hard woman."

The light flickered on as Caroline entered with the trolley. "Sitting in the dark again? Makes me wonder what you two are getting up to. Anyway, let's have supper. I'm famished."

*

Jay left at ten-thirty. They stood on the steps and she said, "This time you *will* phone me?"

He laughed. "Of course. All passion spent, all doubts resolved."

She said softly, "Ring soon, Jay. Very soon."

A breeze mingled with her hair and carried to him that fragrance that had so disturbed him when they were dancing.

She seemed to float towards him in the darkness. Suddenly, she was in his arms. He hugged her once and gently kissed her on the forehead and turned and moved into the night.

He felt a sense of overwhelming joy and his head seemed to be bursting. He started to run at top speed along the dark road.

Chapter Seven

With the last days of October nearly all the leaves dropped and November moved quietly into place, but with a sterner, more puritanical countenance.

It was a fortnight later and Jay lay on his bed and listened to the soft tapping of rain against the window. The door crashed open and Dick entered the room like a fresh wind.

"What a way to spend Saturday afternoon. You should be out and about, enjoying the bracing Yorkshire weather."

Jay made a rude gesture. "That for the bracing Yorkshire weather."

Dick flopped down on his bed. "Now, now, old man. I've never felt better in my life."

"Did you phone Tina?" Jay asked.

"I did indeed, and what do you think? You and the charming Miss Grey are invited to a party by candlelight this evening!"

Jay raised his head and looked across. "Who's giving it?"

"These actors, old man. The group theatre people that Tina belongs to."

Jay laughed shortly. "Sounds great. A lot of broken-down provincial Bohemians. Phoney actors, phoney poets and phoney writers. Cord jackets and beards. No thank you."

"Come on, Jay. You and Caroline have been keeping pretty close to yourselves for the past couple of weeks. You should get out more, mix with people. Besides, you haven't asked her. How do you know she doesn't want to go? She might fancy the idea."

Jay swung his legs to the floor and sat up. "All right, I'll ask her."

He went down to the orderly room to telephone. Jonathan Grey answered and told him that Caroline was not in. She had gone to Haxby to do some shopping. Jay thanked him and hung up. He went back to the room and said, "She's shopping in Haxby. I'll phone her again later."

"Strike while the iron's hot is my motto," Dick said. "If she's in Haxby, we can't miss her. We'll run down in the Jag and ask her together. I don't trust you. You mightn't put it across properly. I want to make sure Miss Grey sees it in its most favourable light."

"Has it got one?" Jay said as they went out.

*

They found Caroline in the village grocer's. Dick waited in the car while Jay went to her. She was standing at the counter with several older women and the grocer was making up her order.

"Hello, angel," Jay said. "When you're ready, we'll run you back to the house."

"You're always bobbing up when I least expect you," she said. "I'll only be a moment. My order's almost ready."

He lit a cigarette and leaned against the side counter. The women looked at him disapprovingly. One middle-aged woman stared icily and he winked slowly and deliberately. She flushed and looked away.

"I'm ready," Caroline said. He picked up her basket and they left the shop. As he closed the door behind him, he heard the buzz of conversation begin.

"Hello," Dick said. "How's my girl?"

Caroline squeezed into the car and Jay put the basket on the rear seat. "The only exercise most of those old girls take is jumping to conclusions."

"Don't mind them," Caroline said. "They just like to gossip. They do it about everybody."

"I think it must be the uniform," Dick said. "Soldier seems to be a dirty word in these parts."

The car roared along the main road out of Haxby and braked at the bottom of the steps leading to the front door of the Greys' house.

"What about tonight?" Caroline asked Jay as she got out.

"That's why we came looking for you. Dick wants us to go to some party in Rainford. All very arty. Beards and candlelight. What do you think?"

"It might be fun," she said. "Yes, I'd like to go."

"What did I tell you?" Dick said. "We'll pick you up around seven."

Jay waved as the car accelerated down the drive and

then he turned to Dick and said, "One thing, if this party turns out to be a dead loss, you've got to bring us back early. Promise?"

"Of course, but you'll love it, old man. Do you a world of good."

Jay settled back in the seat morosely. He didn't want to go to the party. He knew that it would run pretty true to the general pattern of such things. Plenty of beer and much passing of girls from hand-to-hand. Still, if it turned sour, they could always leave, which was some sort of consolation.

*

That evening as they were preparing to go out, there was a phone call for Dick. When he came back, he looked faintly disgruntled.

"Anything wrong?" Jay asked him.

"Tina can't get away until much later than she thought. She wants us to go on to the party without her and she'll come when she can. It doesn't really matter. I know the address anyway."

Jay didn't say anything because he knew that Dick's mind was working overtime, creating for himself the events of the next few hours, convinced already perhaps, that Tina was not coming, that he would face disappointment again.

Caroline was ready and waiting when they called. Dick sounded the horn and she came straight away, looking, in the porch light, incredibly fresh and very young.

Jay handed her into the car. "You look charming to-night. Like a flower. You'll certainly be like a breath of fresh air where we're going."

She flushed and warmth shone in her eyes, deep and secret and for the two of them only. When he squeezed in beside her, she slipped her hand into his arm and whispered, "Life gets better every day." She looked up at the stars. "It's going to be a perfect evening. Just perfect."

As the car turned into the main road, Dick acceler-ated until they were rushing through the night, the wind in their hair.

He started to sing at the top of his voice and Caro-line and Jay joined in. They sang all the way into Rainford. As they passed through the crowded, lighted streets the sound of their voices, gay and young and transitory, touched the ears of the passers-by with an envious sadness.

Dick pulled up in front of the Majestic Hotel. "We might as well have a drink in the lounge for half-an-hour. No point in going to the party too soon. No one will be there until nine at the earliest."

Jay and Caroline got out of the car and went on into the hotel and Dick took the car round to the parking lot at the rear.

"What's the matter with Dick," Caroline said as they went into the lounge.

"You don't miss a thing, do you?" Jay said. "It's his girl. She can't come until later and Dick thinks she must be giving him the air."

"But why should he think that?"

Jay took out his cigarettes and lit one before replying. "He's completely insecure, at least that's how I read him. There must be quite a difference between being the scion of a noble family and the offspring of a self-made grandfather and father. Your natural aristocrat is so sure of himself because of his background of tradition and family, that he seldom feels insecure. Dick knows his only background is money and that probably counted for very little at his prep school and Harrow. He's man the perpetual hunter, with this difference: he hunts for love and affection and reassurance. He never gets it and each experience scars him a little more."

"Perhaps he expects too much too soon. A woman can't be rushed, you know. She has to feel sure."

Dick entered the lounge, his appearance and manner the very antithesis of Jay's description.

"Haven't you ordered, old man?"

"Waiting for you, money bags," Jay said.

Dick laughed delightedly at the insult and waved to a waiter. He ordered an iced fruit-juice for Caroline. "Can't have people accusing us of corrupting the young," he told her.

The conversation flowed easily. Dick and Jay vied with each other in remembering outrageous anecdotes from undergraduate days and they kept Caroline bubbling with laughter for an hour. The only flaw was Dick's repeated nod to the waiter indicating another round.

Jay declined firmly after a couple, but Dick continued alone. When they finally decided to leave, there was already a glitter in his eyes that indicated mischief to come.

The house in which the party was being held was in a dilapidated street distinguished by the name of Cemetery Drive. They parked the car and mounted stone steps to a peeling front door on which Dick hammered cheerfully with the toe of his shoe.

"Georgian, and seen better days," Jay said, craning his neck and looking up at the dim bulk of the house rising three storeys above them.

There was a protesting curse from inside the house and the door was flung open so that it crashed against the wall. They caught a glimpse of a man disappearing back down the corridor, his hair so long that one might have been forgiven for making a mistake.

"Nice of him to let us in," Dick said. "Anyway, in we go, children. This way to iniquity."

The corridor was dimly lit by cheap candles. A tremendous hubbub from the far end indicated the vortex of the party although delighted squeals and sounds of movement from a room on the left suggested that things had already begun to fan out.

They entered the room at the end of the corridor and found themselves on the edge of a noisy, articulate throng of people. Everybody seemed to be talking to everybody else at the tops of their voices.

Again, the light came from candles stuck in old wine-bottles, placed at various strategic points in the room. No-one took the slightest notice of the new arrivals. Dick pushed his way into the thick of the mob and completely disappeared.

"How do you like it?" Jay said.

Caroline shook her head. "Give me time. Perhaps when I've talked to one or two people."

"They'll talk all right," he said cynically. "It's about all most of them can do."

They stood back against the wall and he tried to see Dick in the gloom. Suddenly he burst from the crowd, three drinks balanced in his hands. Closely behind him followed a tall, thin man wearing a beard and corduroy jacket.

"Here you are, kiddies," Dick said. "Drinks on the house. If you want any more, the bar's in the corner over there."

The bearded man said in an affected voice, "I say, Dick, are these your friends?"

"Sorry, Reggie." Dick made a quick introduction. Apparently Reggie was their host.

He held Caroline's hand rather longer than was necessary. "What a nice little girl." He leered unpleasantly at Jay. "Have fun, my dear fellow. Plenty of rooms upstairs and we're all terribly broadminded."

He moved back into the anonymity of the crowd leaving Jay with a strong desire to place a foot firmly in his rear.

"What an unpleasant man," Caroline said.

"Looks to me as if he still isn't very good at distinguishing between the girls and the boys," Jay said.

Dick laughed. "I shouldn't be surprised. I'm going to circulate." He moved away and then turned. "By the way, I wouldn't stray far from Caroline. Some of the blokes here are positive bloody vultures." He grinned pleasantly and turned into the crowd.

"What's in your glass?" Jay asked Caroline.

"It's all right, only orange juice," she said. "Do you think Dick was right?"

"About not leaving you? Most of these people haven't a moral scruple to bless themselves with." He swallowed some beer. "If anyone gets funny, tell me straight away. A swift kick in the right place will do more good than a sermon."

"The girls must be a pretty funny lot?"

"In more ways than one." He finished his beer. "I'll get another and then we'll follow Dick's example and circulate. If we've got to suffer this damned party, then at least we'll complete your education and get some good out of it."

For about half-an-hour they moved through the crowd, pausing here and there to listen to the conversation and sometimes to allow Caroline to see some unusually odd specimen at close quarters.

Jay decided they were the most unsavoury bunch he had seen in a long time. The room now filled completely as more people arrived and late-comers packed the corridor.

Occasionally, they saw Dick and each time his face gleamed a little more brightly and his smile was a little more fixed. Tina had evidently not arrived. Dick recognized them the first time. After that, he didn't seem to be noticing anything except a rather fly-blown young blonde who was gazing into his face with the ardent look of a Cocker Spaniel.

Jay managed to find a spare corner for them to stand in when they had finally tired of moving about. He left Caroline and went to the bar to replenish their glasses. There was quite a crowd and it took him several minutes to get the drinks.

As he returned, he saw that she was engaged in conversation with a man in a tweed sports jacket. He gave Caroline her drink and said belligerently. "She's already spoken for."

The other laughed pleasantly. "Too pretty not to be, so I didn't expect anything. My name's Turner."

Jay realized at once that here was a different specimen from the rest of the men present. "Sorry," he said. "It's just that one has to watch it with some of these bright types."

Turner nodded and offered him a cigarette. He had light-brown hair falling low over a powerful, intelligent brow. The face beneath it was ugly, but with the pleasant ugliness of the Mongolian. Jay wondered whether somewhere far back in his ancestry, there had been an influx of blood from Tartary.

Turner looked at Caroline, "Enjoying yourself?"

"Not really," she said. "Everyone seems to be trying to have a good time instead of having one, if you follow me, There's a desperately fake heartiness about it that's rather awful."

Turner nodded. "Most of them are quite ordinary people by day; office workers, shopworkers and so on. This is how they spend their leisure time. Trying desperately to be what they're not. It's all very sad."

He looked as if he would not have given a damn if the floor had opened up and swallowed the lot of them.

Jay said, "Why, you're actually intelligent. What on earth are you doing at this brawl?"

Turner laughed. "I'm as big a phoney as any of them. I'm a writer and my point of contact with many people here is that I'm also unsuccessful. The difference between us lies in the fact that I really *do* write and that one day I'll be a success. I come to these affairs as seldom as possible and then only to frighten myself into working hard at my novel. The thought of ending up like most of these types serves as a stimulant."

Jay nodded. "I can guess how you feel. It would send me round the bend."

"I see you're in Intelligence," Turner said. "Where are you stationed?"

Jay told him and before long, they had drifted on to history and a discussion of its place in the modern world. Caroline mostly listened, putting in an odd word now and then.

After a while, there was a pause in the conversation and Turner said, "So you come from London, eh? How do you find the industrial North. Are they any more broadminded up here than they are in Notting Hill?"

"You wouldn't think so, the way we seem to make people talk," Caroline put in.

"We must be charitable," Jay said. "Most people are pretty decent, I think."

Turner's face cracked into a sardonic smile. "If that's your attitude, you're licked before you start because you've misjudged the enemy. You say that the bulk of people are decent, even kindly. Well, they're not. The average Englishman is the most damnable hypocrite in the world. Underneath his surface kindliness, he's more intolerant than a Kentucky colonel."

"That's pretty damning," Jay said. "It certainly doesn't give people in our position much hope."

"Just a minute, Jay," Caroline was completely serious and her voice was earnest as she said, "What can we do, Mr Turner? if that's all there is for us, what ought we to do?"

The noise and the oppressive atmosphere seemed to recede and the three of them were in a vacuum of quiet as Turner said gravely, "There's only one thing you can do. Enjoy yourselves tonight. If you meet tomorrow, enjoy that also. Happiness is only relative; that's the great secret of life. If you're happy Now, you can't have more than that, even if you have each other for twenty years."

The noise of the room enfolded them again, but Caroline was smiling in a peculiar, contented way and she squeezed Jay's hand and said, "I've had enough. Let's find Dick and go."

Jay nodded and said good night to Turner, but the

man barely smiled, already withdrawn once more into himself, secure from external forces.

Caroline wanted to go to the bathroom before they went and Jay went upstairs with her and waited on the landing. When she came out, they turned to go back downstairs when a bedroom door on their left opened and the young bonde sauntered out and went into the bathroom.

A second later, Dick emerged. He looked ill and his face was like a death mask, but he managed a weak smile.

"You damned fool," Jay said. "What did you expect to find in there?"

The smile fell from Dick's face and he looked naked and alone and utterly found out. He staggered, almost falling over the banisters and Jay grabbed at him quickly and helped him slowly downstairs.

"I'll drive," he said to Caroline. "He'd get us all killed in this state."

As they approached the door that led to the street, it opened and a pretty and vivacious young woman entered. She paused for a moment at the sight of Dick and then moved forward quickly.

"Dick, you fool. What have you been up to?"

Dick opened a bleary eye and croaked, "Tina? Why didn't you come? You said you would come." And then he passed out.

The girl seemed distressed. "I tried to get here earlier," she said, "but I couldn't get away any sooner tonight. I just couldn't."

Caroline smiled. "I wouldn't waste any breath on him. He can't hear you, I'm afraid. I'm Caroline Grey and this is Jay Williams. I suppose you've heard about us. Anyway, we'll take him home. I don't know if you want to stay. If you do, you're made of sterner stuff than I am."

"Gladly give you a lift," Jay said.

Tina nodded. "Thanks a lot. I hate these affairs. It was Dick who was keen to come, not me. I've been to too many of them."

Jay laid Dick out in the rear seat and the three of them got into the front. Tina lived fairly near in an unpretentious working-class neighbourhood. They dropped her at her door and she thanked them and asked Jay to tell Dick she would phone him the next day.

Jay took it easy on the Haxby road and tried to light a cigarette with one hand. Caroline finally took pity on him and lit it for him.

"Tina seems to be a very nice girl," she said.

Jay nodded. "I'm amazed. She's not Dick's usual type at all. I'd say she's very level-headed and sensible. A girl like that would do him some good."

"Do I do *you* some good?" she said as she got out of the car.

He grinned. "I have no statement to make at this time. See you tomorrow."

*

When they reached Greystones, he parked the car and carried Dick up to their room across his shoulders.

He laid him on the bed, unloosened his tie and took off his shoes. He carefully covered him with a blanket and said softly, "There, my dear comrade. Sleep it off and God help you."

Dick moved a little, groaned and then said quite distinctly, "Tina?"

Jay smiled and said to the sprawling figure. "Perhaps there *is* hope for you after all."

He turned off the light and lay in the dark, smoking a cigarette, thinking.

Chapter Eight

Dick hardly seemed to be affected the next day. He slept through breakfast and got up about ten and had a shower. He and Jay had lunch in Haxby and his appetite seemed unimpaired.

They were working hard together over a Russian grammar when someone called him to the telephone. When he returned to the room, he was smiling broadly and began to change.

"Going out?" Jay said.

"That was Tina. She explained about last night. Her parents were late getting back from a visit to relatives and she was looking after her two young brothers. I think I'll take her to a show tonight."

"What about some Russian verbs for a change?"

"Not enough competition," Dick said as he went out of the door.

Jay passed an industrious afternoon and then went to Caroline's for tea. He was back at Greystones and already in bed at eleven when Dick came in.

"I've had a wonderful idea for next Saturday."

"Not another one," Jay said. "I should have thought last night's fiasco would have cured you."

"Give me a chance, Jay. It's a good idea. If the weather is anything like as mild as it's been these last few days, we'll take a drive to the coast, the four of us. I know a fellow in Rainford who has a bungalow on the cliffs near Flamborough. Lovely spot. We can take some grub and make a day of it. What do you say?"

Jay smiled. "I'll ask Caroline."

"Then it's settled," Dick said as he put out the light. "She's game for anything."

*

Caroline accepted enthusiastically and started making arrangements about food almost straight away. Early on the following Saturday morning, Dick drove into Rainford to pick up Tina and then returned to Caroline's house where he had already left Jay. They loaded the car and set off in high spirits with Jonathan Grey waving from the top of the steps.

It was a glorious day and unbelievably for November, the sun appeared in an almost cloudless blue sky before they had been on the road for long. They sang and shouted all the way to the coast, not stopping until they reached their destination.

The bungalow was a simple wooden building, but its situation was magnificent and the view of the sea, breathtaking.

The girls cooked lunch and afterwards, they all drove into Bridlington and had a look round. Most of the cafés and shops were closed for the winter. There was the silent and rather deserted feeling that one always finds in holiday resorts out of season. After an hour or so, Jay suggested they should go back to the bungalow.

"I see there's a dance on tonight," Dick said. "What about going?"

Jay glanced at Caroline and she shook her head slightly. "Sorry, Dick, we're not keen."

"Would you like to go, Tina?" Dick said.

"Oh, I would," she said with enthusiasm, "as long as Caroline and Jay don't mind being on their . . ."

"You and Tina go, Dick," Caroline said. "You can't stay very late, anyway. You can come back to the bungalow for us when you're ready to go home."

"You're an angel," Dick told her. "We'll do just that."

When they reached the bungalow, he suggested they go inside and play some records. Caroline said no firmly. "Jay and I want to go for a walk along the cliffs," and she took him by the hand and pulled him away.

"What's the idea?" Jay demanded when they got outside.

"They want to be on their own," she said. "Can't you see how much Dick likes her and that she thinks the world of him."

"Sorry, but I haven't got any feminine intuition. They looked perfectly normal to me."

The blue sky dipped away over the sea to touch the

horizon and the sun was warm on their skin. "What an incredible day for November."

"Isn't it what they call a St. Martin's Summer?" Caroline said. "I read about it somewhere. Pretty rare, though."

He stopped to light a cigarette. When he raised his head, she had moved ahead of him to the edge of the cliff. She turned and came back, but for a moment, fear had touched him.

She moved through the dry grass and the sun was behind her. The image blurred at the edges until, when she paused for a moment and looked out to sea again, she might have been a painting by one of the impressionists.

She looked unreal and etheral and completely and utterly transitory as if at any moment she might fly away. As soon as she spoke, the spell was broken.

"Let's sit for a while, Jay."

They flung themselves down in the long grass. After a while, he closed his eyes and relaxed. It was pleasant, so pleasant, to lie in the sun with the right person and just to do nothing.

He decided there was a lot to be said for beachcombing. Something tickled his nose. He opened his eyes and caught Caroline gently stroking him with a blade of grass.

"Penny for them," she said.

"It occurred to me that it might be nice to be a beachcomber."

She laughed softly. ". . . on some South Sea island

with girls in grass skirts weaving garlands for your neck. Men are all the same."

He closed his eyes. Her voice moved on, began to rise and fall and then it became a steady murmur that melted into the timeless, sad sough of the sea.

*

He awakened suddenly. Above him, clouds turned and wheeled across the sky and hinted at a break in the weather. She had gone. He scrambled to his feet and looked about him. There was no sign of her. A slight twinge of panic sent him running to the edge of the cliff and then he saw her down on the beach at the water's edge.

A crazily tilted path fell away beneath him and he stepped on to it and began a careful descent. She was standing knee-deep in the sea and she held the skirt of her frock bunched in front of her with one hand while she scrabbled in the water with the other.

Jay approached quietly, picked up a stone and threw it so that it splashed her slightly when it landed.

"Oh, you beast!" she said and waded out of the water towards him.

"You deserted me," he told her. "I awakened to find you had vanished like an enchanted princess in some fairy tale."

She carried her sandals in one hand and slipped the other into his arm and they walked along the beach, back towards the bungalow.

"I wish it was like a fairy tale," she said. "I wish

this was an enchanted day standing still in time and that you and I were together for ever and ever."

There was a depth, a poignancy to her voice that he had never heard before. It was strangely disturbing.

"Remember what Turner said last Saturday?" Jay said. "About being happy for the moment and how that was all anyone could ever count on? He was right. People in love exist in the eternal Now. The trouble is that philosophies like his satisfy nobody because love is transitory and carries its own sadness."

She stood quiet still and her eyes were shining, glowing with a great warmth. "You said people in love," she told him. "Did you mean it?"

"Fifteen-year-old girls aren't supposed to fall in love," he said, "and certainly not with men like me."

They started to walk again and she hugged his arm and her voice bubbled with happiness. "I don't care what people think. It's none of their business. I only want them to leave us alone."

"They never do, that's the trouble with life," he said.

They scrambled up a path to the top of the cliffs and Caroline said she was going to a farm several fields away to see if she could get some milk. She told Jay to make a loud noise when approaching the bungalow and to ask Tina to start getting tea ready. She gave him a brief smile and then ran very fast across the fields like a young boy.

He did as he was told and sang a snatch of a popular song as he drew near the bungalow. When he entered,

Dick grinned amiably. "Very considerate, but I bet *you* didn't think of it."

Jay ignored him and said to Tina, "Caroline's gone for some milk. She wondered if you'd start getting tea ready."

Tina nodded and went into the small kitchen and Dick put on a record and beat time to the music with a fork from the table. He looked gay and untroubled and completely happy.

Jay wandered outside and stood looking across the fields towards the farm. As clouds moved across the sun, a great belt of shadow spilled darkness like a fast-spreading stain across the ground.

He saw Caroline moving towards him and he started to run because for some incomprehensible reason, he felt a desperate urgency to reach her before the shadow did.

When he was still thirty or forty yards away, it enveloped her and he stopped running. And then the shadow passed over him in turn and he felt suddenly chilled. For the second time that day, he knew fear.

She waved to him and he saw that she carried a milk can in one hand. He walked to meet her and took the can and they moved back to the bungalow together.

"Why were you running?" she said.

He searched desperately for a convincing explanation and said lamely, "I suddenly felt energetic, that's all."

Dick and Tina had things well under way and they all sat down to tea at once. Dick was impatient to be off. "The dance starts at seven," he said. "We can only stay a couple of hours so let's get there as soon as possible."

After the meal was finished he hardly gave Tina time to fix her make-up before he was hustling her out. "We'll be back about nine-thirty," he called. "Have fun kiddies."

The sound of the engine faded into the distance and quiet fell about them.

"What shall we do?" Jay said.

"Play some music. Just enjoy being alone together."

He put some records on the gramophone and they moved across to a divan placed by a double glass window that looked over the sea. Caroline sat down and he swung his legs up and lay with his head in her lap.

"You don't need to move," he said. "That thing holds twelve records and I've filled it." He closed his eyes. "This is nice. This is very nice."

She stroked his hair gently with one hand. "What's going to become of us, Jay?"

"What do you mean?"

"One of these days you'll finish at Greystones, won't you?"

"Next summer. I think the end-of-course exams will be held sometime in June. That's a long way off though."

"Will you be sent abroad?"

"Very improbable. I'll only have about six months service left to do. They might send me to Germany."

"Will you forget me?"

She put the question lightly. Yet he realized she trembled on the edge of an abyss of loneliness.

"If I never saw you again after today, I'd remember everything about you for the rest of my life."

He still had his eyes closed as he waited for her reply. He heard a choked sob and opened them and looked up into her face. Tears were running down her cheeks and her face was contorted with grief.

"Caroline, what is it?" He twisted round to face her.

She pressed a hand against her cheek. "Oh, Jay," she said brokenly. "If you ever left me, I don't know what I'd do. I'd never feel complete again."

Her tear-stained face was lifted up to him. Instinctively and naturally and for the first time, he kissed her with a quiet passion that was almost frightening in its power.

He leaned back against the divan and cradled her in his arms. She sighed contentedly. "You're so strong. When you kissed me, I felt as though I was going to burst into flames."

He dropped a kiss on her hair. "That side is least important of all. I'd love you if you were in a wheelchair."

For a little while, they were quiet and then she said, "Mrs Brown had the nerve to speak to grandfather about us the other day."

"You didn't tell me."

"I didn't think it was important. She said the whole

village was talking. That my mother would never have approved."

"What did old Jonathan have to say?"

"He told her either to mind her own business or find another job."

Jay lit a cigarette and said, "Don't you notice anything?" She shook her head. "The music's stopped." He got up, went over to the gramophone and turned the records over.

It was completely dark in the room now and he could barely see her silhouetted against the window. She moved towards him, he took her in his arms and they danced until the records were finished. Afterwards, he suggested a stroll and they went outside.

There was a full moon and the sky was clear and a luminosity hung over the sea. Far below, the waves gleamed whitely as they creamed over the rocks. There was a slight chill in the air and he slipped his jacket around her shoulders. They didn't speak at all and after a while, they went back to the bungalow and sat on the divan in the darkness.

*

Very much later as she slept with her head against his chest, he heard the fast approaching hum of the Jaguar. He tried to ease his cramped arm and Caroline stirred and said sleepily, "What time is it? I wish the night would never end. I wish people would pass us by for ever."

"I'm afraid the world's just caught up with us again," he whispered as the Jaguar swept into the track outside.

Dick and Tina were in high spirits. Apparently they had had a wonderful time and Jay noticed there wasn't the usual smell of alcohol on his friend's breath.

It was a day for surprises. They packed up the gear and Dick put up the hood as the night air would be cold on the drive back.

He and Tina sat in the front seat and sang, laughed and joked most of the way into Rainford, behaving in fact like a couple of people in love. Jay and Caroline were silent in the back seat and she lay in the hollow of his arm.

He felt suddenly flat and deflated. There was something wrong. He could think of nothing bright or pleasant. Caroline adored him! Caroline loved him!

For no apparent reason there came to mind an old Greek tag from his classical studies. "For every joy the Gods give two sorrows." How many sorrows would they give him? Did they take into account the greatness of the joy? There was no answer.

They swirled through the streets of Rainford and pulled up outside Tina's house. Dick walked her to the door and there was a murmur of conversation, silence and then more conversation. He returned, whistling cheerfully.

"Wipe the lipstick off," Caroline told him.

"I probably never will," he said as he drove away. "Set up a new fashion."

*

It was late when they turned into the drive of Caroline's house and the place was in darkness. Jay glanced at his watch.

"Good lord, it's past two. I didn't realize it was quite so late."

"You might as well come in for a cup of tea," Caroline said. "I'm making one anyway. It'll save you the trouble of messing about when you get back."

They entered the house by the back door, making as little noise as possible and went into the kitchen. Dick and Jay leaned against the draining board and kept well out of Caroline's way as she started to cut some sandwiches. Jay was holding a match for Dick's cigarette when the door opened and a woman entered.

Somewhere in her late thirties, dressed in an expensive brocade housecoat, her face was cold and hard.

"Caroline," she said, "I want you to go to your room."

Caroline stood as if turned to stone, the breadknife still firmly gripped in one hand. "Mother!" she said in a shocked voice. "What are *you* doing here?"

"Go to bed, Caroline. This instant. No arguments."

Caroline glanced at Jay, her face white and frightened. He smiled and said softly, "Do as your mother says. I'll see you tomorrow."

Margaret Grey looked at Dick and Jay in a detached

116

sort of way and then she walked over to the outside door and opened it.

"You'll oblige me by going, now."

They walked to the door and Dick moved on ahead. She put a hand on Jay's arm. "I'd like to see you tomorrow afternoon. Three o'clock would be all right, I think. You're not on duty on Sunday, I presume?"

"I'm not on duty, Mrs Grey," he said.

"Tomorrow at three then." She closed the door in his face.

"Do you think you'll be able to handle her?" Dick said as they drove away.

"I think so," Jay told him.

But he did not. Not for one minute. It was as if something big and black and terrible was hurrying towards him, great talons ready to tear his soul to pieces as payment for the happiness he had stolen.

Chapter Nine

Jay tossed and turned uneasily for the rest of the night. It was approaching dawn before he finally fell asleep. He was awakened by Dick with a cup of coffee.

"What time is it?"

"Almost noon. I thought I'd let you sleep. You were moaning and groaning for most of the night."

Jay fumbled for a cigarette and sat up in bed, his back against the wall. The coffee tasted fine and the cigarette was rough and sharp—just what he needed.

"You look worried," Dick said.

Jay tried to grin, but somehow, it didn't come off.

"Let's face facts. This whole thing is about to blow up in my face. You warned me in the beginning that something like this could happen."

Dick shrugged. "I don't see what she can do. After all, you haven't been getting up to fun and games. She can't get you for corruption or anything."

Jay swallowed the rest of his coffee and then swung his legs to the floor and stood up. "It's not myself I'm worried about. What effect is all this going to have on Caroline? Heaven only knows what her mother has up her sleeve for three o'clock this afternoon."

"A six-shooter, I shouldn't wonder," Dick said and laughed. "Oh, damn it all, Jay. It's obvious to anyone with half an eye that you and Caroline are deeply attached to each other. Once she realizes that, she'll look at the whole thing in a different light."

"You think so?" Jay shook his head. "Not if old Jonathan's description of her is anything to go by."

He reached for his dressing gown and towel and left the room.

*

It was about two o'clock when Jay set out. Dick had wanted to give him a lift for he was driving into Rainford to see Tina, but he had preferred to walk.

Walking was slower and it therefore took him longer to reach his destination. A cowardly procrastination, but he was beginning to feel scared.

It was all piling up inside him—the emotion and the fears and the old neurotic conviction that the world was against them because they had dared to disturb the ordered pattern of things. He started to sweat. Panic flickered in his stomach.

He was passing through Haxby at the time and he dropped into The Tall Man and had a quick drink to steady his nerves. When he left, he was not afraid any longer. He felt calm and drained of all emotion, ready for what was to come.

When he walked up the drive, Digby the Labrador, came tearing round the corner as he had done on that first day. This time, the barks changed to whimpers of pleasure. Jay stood at the bottom of the steps and fondled the animal for a moment. Then the door opened and Mrs Brown emerged.

"Will you come in please, sir?"

He paused in the doorway and looked directly into her eyes. She coloured and he smiled gently and walked on into the house.

"In here Mr Williams, if you please." Margaret Grey's voice seemed controlled, but rather remote.

Jay stood just inside the room. She was sitting by the window, perfectly groomed, apparently in complete control of the situation. Old Jonathan was in his chair by the fire, one of his evil-smelling cheroots clamped between his teeth. There was no sign of Caroline.

Jay ignored Margaret Grey. He walked over to the old man and said, "Got one of those to spare?"

A tiny smile flickered at the corners of Jonathan Grey's mouth. "Help yourself, my boy."

Jay lit the cheroot, then walked over to the piano, sat down and started to play.

Margaret Grey looked annoyed. Her face was very white and her eyes sparkled angrily. Before she could say anything, Caroline spoke from the door.

"Hello, Jay." Her voice was quiet and subdued and yet she was unable to keep the gladness from it.

He stopped playing, swung round on the piano stool and held out his hands. She came straight to him without looking at her mother.

120

He turned to Margaret Grey and said, "Well?"

She smiled tightly. "What do you expect me to do. Give you my blessing?"

She stood up and crossing the room in a few swift strides, caught Caroline by the arm and pulled her away from him. "Do you think I'm going to let my daughter shame me like this? The whole village is talking. My daughter, a fifteen-year-old schoolgirl running around with a . . . with a . . ."

She floundered for words and Jay said gently, "With a what, Mrs Grey? What am I?"

She ignored the remark and turned to Jonathan. "As for you," she said, "You actually condoned the whole business."

The old man chuckled. "Why not? There was no harm in it."

"I might have expected as much from you. You always have taken this kind of line—all through your life."

Caroline moved quickly past her mother, back to Jay's side. "I love Jay, mother. He's been very good to me."

Margaret Grey took a cigarette from a silver box on the table and lit it. She blew out a long column of smoke, apparently calm again, and said dryly, "I'm sure he has. Don't worry. I've seen my lawyer. Mr Williams won't be laughing much longer."

Jay slowly and carefully stubbed out the cheroot. His hands were trembling slightly and the palms were beginning to sweat.

"Don't tell me you're going to have us all in the Sunday papers, Mrs Grey?"

"They have a flair for dealing with men who take advantage of fifteen-year-old girls. They put them out of harm's way for rather a long period."

Caroline tried to speak, but Jay cut in quickly. "Is that supposed to be some kind of threat?"

"That depends on you." She moved across to the fire and spread her hands to its warmth. "I don't want a scandal. I just want you to go away and leave my daughter alone."

"And if I refuse?"

"Then I'll have every right to take proceedings. Caroline is under age, remember. I don't know what the penalty would be, but I'm quite sure it would effectively rule out any hopes you may have of a university career."

"There hasn't been anything between them that would warrant legal proceedings," Jonathan said.

"It's hardly likely that *you* would have noticed, even if it had happened right under your nose."

Caroline stepped forward quickly. "There's been enough of this, mother." Her face was very white and her hands tightly clenched. "You're not going to make trouble for Jay. If you do, I'll make you look silly and that's something you can't stand, isn't it?"

"What do you mean?" Margaret Grey's voice was quiet, but a tiny line had appeared between her eyes.

"If you take Jay to court, I'll deny he ever touched me. I'll demand a medical examination."

There was utter silence for a second or two as the full impact of her words sunk in. Then her mother leaned forward and slapped her heavily across the face.

Jay pulled her violently away. He turned and gathered Caroline into his arms. She was crying as he led her from the room.

They went out of the back door and he guided her towards the summer house that stood at the far end of the garden. She cried for several minutes and he held her against his chest and gently stroked her hair. Gradually, she began to get control of herself.

Jay took out his cigarettes. "Have one," he said. "It'll do you good."

She held the cigarette between fingers that trembled slightly and puffed at it in her inexpert way until the smoke caught in her throat and she began to cough.

When she finally managed to catch her breath, she laughed shakily. "That's better. That's much better." She tried to smile but failed miserably. There was only tragedy in her eyes when she said, "Wasn't it awful?"

"God gives us our relations, our friends we make ourselves." He said the old tag lightly, but her only response was a despondent little shrug of the shoulders.

"What do you think she'll do?"

He looked up at the house and wondered if Mrs Grey was watching them. "She can't make any real trouble. You've effectively scotched that."

"But I'm worried, Jay. Worried about what she might try to do to you." Caroline's voice had a desperate intensity to it.

"There's nothing she can do to me. At most, she can have me warned to stay away from you. If she doesn't approve of me, she has a right to do that. After all, you *are* under age."

He fumbled for a cigarette and sighed. "I should imagine she'll take the simple solution."

"What's that?"

"She'll take you back to London with her."

Caroline jumped up. "I shan't go. She can't make me."

He pulled her down beside him. "Yes, she can. You're only fifteen. The law says you must live with your legal guardian or parents until you're sixteen. After that age, you can leave home and the only rights she'll possess are certain legal ones such as permission to get married and things like that."

There was a faint shadow under her eyes. "But I don't want to go. I want to stay here."

He shook his head. "You've really got to grow up in the next few minutes. You've got to listen to what I say and accept it. Whatever is between you and me at the moment has to have the world's approval and that includes your mother."

"But what are we going to do?" Her voice was high-pitched, insistent.

"If necessary, you must go to London with her. I'll have to stay on here. When you're sixteen, you can insist on living with your grandfather. She can't do anything about that. Not unless she can prove you're in need of care and protection." He squeezed her hand. "It's the only way out. There isn't anything I can do."

She took a deep breath and smiled bravely. "All right, Jay. If you say so, I'll live with her. I'll do as she says until my birthday. But after that . . ."

"Good girl," he said. "Don't worry. I'll write to you. Perhaps I can get a forty-eight hour pass some weekend and come down to see you. She can't watch you all the time."

"That would be lovely," Caroline said. Her voice was tired and played out, like a record running down.

"We'd better go back and see what she's up to."

As they walked up to the house, Caroline slipped her hand into his arm. "One thing I'm glad about. She can't harm you. That's the important thing."

A slight feeling of unease stirred inside him. She can't harm me—or can she? The thought stayed with him as they entered the back door and walked through to the lounge.

Jonathan Grey was still in his chair by the fire. There was no sign of Mrs Grey. The old man smiled crookedly as they entered. "Damnable woman, eh, my boy?"

"Where is she?" Jay said.

"Packing. I'm afraid she's taking Caroline back to London with her this evening. I heard her phoning for a taxi. I don't think you two have much time left."

"We know, grandfather." Caroline ran forward and dropped on her knees at his side. "Jay guessed she would. I'm going to go without any fuss. We mustn't have any more trouble. But I'm coming back as soon as I can. You'll let me come back, won't you?"

The old man gently ruffled her hair. "Of course I will, my darling. Just as soon as it can be arranged."

Margaret Grey spoke from the door. "Very touching."

Jay turned towards her. "Isn't life ironic, Mrs Grey. On paper, my qualifications are fine. Young and healthy, a Ph.D. at twenty-three. Ordinarily, if you'd heard your daughter had a thing about me, you'd have smiled indulgently and asked me to take it a little easy. Amazing what a difference the colour of a man's skin can make."

She seemed about to say something in reply when a car horn sounded in the drive outside. "The taxi," she said. "At least we don't have to drag this farce out. I've packed an overnight bag for you, Caroline. We're leaving now. There's a train from Rainford at five-thirty. I intend to be on it."

Caroline stood up and her mother held out a coat to her. Jay moved forward quickly and took it. He smiled quietly and Caroline slipped her arms into the sleeves.

"Thank you, Jay." It was almost a whisper.

They walked out into the hall and he picked up the cases. "Allow me, Mrs Grey," he said pleasantly.

It was soon over. Caroline got into the back of the

taxi. Just before she sat down, she turned and looked at him. He smiled reassuringly.

Margaret Grey got in and closed the door. She spoke to the driver and the car moved away. There was a brief glimpse of Caroline's agonized white face at the rear window and then the car turned out of the gates into the main road.

*

There was silence. After a while, Jay turned to Jonathan Grey who stood in the doorway. "How did she find out?"

"Father Costello wrote to her."

"Why, for God's sake?"

"He thought it was for the best, I suppose."

"They create the problem for themselves," Jay said. "All of them. Why can't they see that?" He laughed harshly. "I'll tell you something, Mr Grey. I worked my guts out to move from the Portobello Road into a calmer, more ordered world. Nobody's called me nigger for years, but they still manage to make their point."

"Come and have a drink," the old man said.

*

They had their drink. They had several and when Jay left he no longer felt afraid. Only angry—at Margaret Grey and at the world.

He was just coming into Haxby when the Jaguar stopped beside him. "Get in!" Dick said.

Jay found to his surprise that he had some difficulty in opening the door. Dick obliged and Jay collapsed into the seat. "Where's Tina?"

"I was worried about you. She could tell, so she ordered me to come and find out what was happening. I thought it would be all over by now."

"It's over, all right."

"What happened?"

"She didn't like me. Threatened to take proceedings if I didn't fade out of the picture."

"The lousy bitch. What did she do? Kick you out."

"Oh, no, I'm stronger than she is. She simply folded her tents like the Arabs and stole away. She's taken Caroline with her."

"To London?"

"Correct!" Jay was at that stage of drunkenness when the greatest importance is attached to words and their exact meaning. "She has taken her fair young daughter away from my corrupting influence."

Dick took a quick sideways glance. "You're feeling no pain, are you? What exactly have you been drinking?"

"Irish whiskey it said on the bottle. I think old Jonathan must have made it himself."

"The place for you is bed, my lad," Dick said. "You can start worrying tomorrow."

As Jay got out of the car at Greystones, a wave of nausea hit him. He lurched to the kitchen door and leaned against it, desperately trying to keep his senses. Dick hurried up behind and slipped an arm around his shoulders.

"I've got you. In we go."

They negotiated the back stairs successfully and turned along the corridor to their room. As they passed the bathroom, Jay stopped and said carefully, "Just a minute, Dick. Got to pay a call."

He just managed to reach the basin before his stomach heaved and he was violently sick. After a while, he turned on the tap and sloshed cold water over his face.

Dick handed him a towel. "Any better?"

Jay smiled weakly. "I'm a bloody fool, Dick. I'll be all right when I've had a lie down."

They were about to enter their room when a voice called from the end of the corridor, "Williams, I want you!"

It was Sergeant Grant. He was wearing battledress and his dress cap and looked as though he was on duty.

He moved forward and took an exaggeratedly deep breath. "You smell like a distillery. Anyway, fit or not, the colonel wants to see you in ten minutes so get into your best battledress and make it snappy."

"What's the colonel want with him?" Dick said. "It's Sunday."

"He just wants a little chat. That's if you don't mind, *Mister* Kerr," Grant said sarcastically.

Jay's head felt as if it might explode at any moment.

He did not worry about why the colonel might want to see him because for some reason, his mind was numb. He fumbled his way into his uniform, Dick helping him. Grant stood in the doorway and smoked a cigarette.

"I'm ready, Sergeant," he said at last.

"You'd better come with him, Kerr," Grant said. "He don't look too steady on his pins to me."

They went downstairs to the orderly room and Jay and Dick stood outside in the corridor and Grant went in.

"What's all this about?" Dick said anxiously. "It smells fishy to me."

The door opened and Grant stepped out. "Williams!" he barked. "Attention! Quick march!"

Jay obeyed subconsciously. It was with a faint sense of surprise that he found himself in front of the colonel's desk.

Colonel Fitzgerald was examining some papers. "Stand at ease, Williams," he said without looking up.

There was complete silence in the room except for the low buzz of an electric air conditioner in the window. Jay gazed out over the colonel's head.

The trees were stripped bare of all leaves now and the untidy nests of the rookery were clearly exposed to view. He watched a rook flap lazily through the air from one tree to another and then realized the colonel was addressing him.

"I beg your pardon, sir."

Fitzgerald said, "I've been looking at your record. I must confess I find myself utterly bewildered by your disgraceful conduct."

"I don't understand, sir."

"I've had a long telephone conversation with a lady who told me a shocking story. It would seem you've been annoying her fifteen-year-old daughter with your attentions—her fifteen-year-old daughter, a mere child."

"You must be referring to my girl friend, sir." Jay said. "She's the only fifteen-year-old I know. She never said I was annoying her, though. I must ask her next time I see her."

He rocked slightly, heel-and-toe and almost fell down.

"You're drunk," Colonel Fitzgerald said in horror. "Is he drunk, Sergeant Grant?"

"Yes, sir!" Grant answered obediently.

"Put him on a charge," said the colonel. "As for this other matter, you'll leave this young girl alone. You're a disgrace to the British Army."

"Why only the British, sir?" Jay said politely. "Would they approve in the French?"

The colonel's face went purple. "Sergeant Grant." His voice cracked. "Place this man under close arrest."

"Thank you, sir," Jay said. He did an abrupt about-turn, almost fell flat on his face and stumbled into the corridor.

He had a vision of Dick's worried face and then

Grant's loomed largely as he came close.

"Had yourself a nice little bit of young stuff, eh?" He shook his head. "Tell me, Williams. What have you lot got that we haven't?"

Everything went quiet for Jay. There was no sound, only Grant's face very close and the stupid, fleshy mouth under the moustache, opening and closing, and the filthy leer.

"This is what you do if a man is stupid enough to let you get close." Grant had said that and Grant had drummed it into them. *"This is what you do."*

Jay lifted his foot and then, as Grant doubled over, raised his knee into the unprotected face and brought down his fist.

There was a great noise and somebody shouted. It was Dick. Dick was shouting and then the colonel. After that, many voices, all swelling up into a confused murmur. He saw them carry Grant off, his face all bloody, the nose broken and twisted and then they led him away.

*

He went quietly. He was no trouble. No trouble at all. At the court martial, he was a model prisoner and hardly said a word except to thank them when they sentenced him to three months' detention.

He was surprised at the lightness of the sentence, but then he was coloured, which helped. They took him away in handcuffs through the crowded railway station at Rainford with the people staring and they sat in a reserved compartment all the way to the place where they took men like him.

Chapter Ten

A cold wind lifted across the parade ground and there was a hint of rain in the heavy grey clouds beyond the barracks. Jay trudged across the square carrying the kitbag and unwieldy pack that held his equipment.

A brightly-painted sign indicated the 98th Holding Unit and he followed its pointing arrow round behind the barrack block. Facing him were three dilapidated Nissen huts, sad relics of the war years.

He entered the middle hut and found himself in a dimly-lit and sour-smelling room containing a dozen or so army cots. A figure stirred on the one in the far corner.

"Is this the 98th?" Jay said.

There was a groan and a creaking of springs. "Yes, rot your luck, old man. Germany-bound like the rest of us?"

Jay dropped his kit on the floor with a crash and moved forward. "That you, Dick?"

The figure on the bed straightened and then stood up and rushed forward. "Jay, you old bastard. I thought you were never going to get here. I've bribed my way off two drafts already." He gave him an involuntary hug. "When did you get out?"

"Yesterday," Jay told him. "I was given movement orders to report here. Did you say Germany?"

Dick nodded. "Field Security. Berlin, I think."

They sat on the bed and lit cigarettes. "Pretty cold in here," Jay said.

"We use a week's supply of coke in one night. You know the army. February is still July to them as far as fuel supplies go."

"What happened, Dick? Why are you in on this effort?"

"Courtesy of Colonel Fitzgerald. He never forgave me for being such an able witness on your behalf. He bided his time until the mid-course exam. I didn't do so good and he had me thrown out. They're sending all the spare Intelligence types here these days. I've been hanging around for a fortnight. I heard you were due in from a corporal in the records office."

"The one who kept you off two drafts?"

Dick grinned. ". . . for a consideration."

"What do we do all day? What happens?"

"Nothing much. We just hang around, get issued with new kit. Have a few jabs from the M.O. Nobody bothers us. At the moment there are only two other chaps and they've nipped out for the afternoon. I usually do that. Slip out through the Camp Hospital gate and go to the flicks or something."

Jay stood up. "I'll take this bed next to you," he

said. "I'll unpack my kit and then how about you and I taking the afternoon off. I could do with a decent meal for one thing, and a drink—in fact several."

"Why wait to unpack?" Dick said. "You can do that later. We'll go now."

They went out through the hospital gate and walked down the main road towards the centre of Aldershot. Dick kept staring at Jay as though he was seeing him for the first time.

"My God," he finally said. "What did they do to you?"

"I don't want to talk about it. It's all over now, Dick. All over." Jay gave a tight nervous smile. "You've no idea what a wonderful sensation it is to be walking down a street like this. When I was travelling here, I felt the same way. A sense of space and freedom."

"What you need is a damned good meal and your uncle Dick's the man to provide that."

Ten minutes later they were sitting at a table in the best hotel in town. "I'll have a steak," Jay said. "A big, thick one, plenty of potatoes and mixed vegetables. That'll do for a start."

They talked very little during the meal as he made up for the semi-starvation of the past months. It was over coffee and a cigarette that they really exchanged news.

"Did you get my letters?" Dick said.

"I got two letters all the time I was in there. One from you and the other—this will give you a laugh—

the other from the firm I sent my manuscript to. They're going to publish."

"Bloody good show!" Dick said. "You'll be famous yet. I'll be getting invitations to parties a few years from now, just because I know you."

Jay stirred his coffee very slowly and carefully. "What happened, Dick? I haven't heard a word."

"It's not so good, Jay. She's in a convent school in Richmond. I got it from Jonathan. He couldn't write to you and I didn't know what to tell you, so I didn't mention it in my letters. Anyway, I wrote several. What happened to them?"

Jay shrugged. "They don't bother too much in those places. Sometimes you get them, sometimes you don't."

"I tried to see her, Jay. I really tried, but you can imagine what it must be like. Probably she even has her mail censored."

"I've got to see her again before I leave," Jay said and there was a quiet desperation in his voice. "I've become the world for her. If she loses me, she'll think she's lost everything. She must have been going through hell for the past three months."

"We'll work something out," Dick said, "but we'll have to move fast. I don't know the exact date we're leaving, but it won't be any longer than a week or ten days. We're flying out, you know."

Jay lit another cigarette and drummed nervously with his fingers on the table. "I've just got to see her, even if it means breaking into the damned place. I couldn't stand having her think I'd let her down."

Dick could find nothing to say. He called for the bill and they left. As they were walking along the main street, they passed a garage and he said suddenly, "Just a minute, Jay. I've got an idea."

He went in, leaving Jay standing on the pavement. He was back in a couple of minutes. "Just the job," he said. "My car's in London, but I've just asked the bloke in here if he can hire me one for the day. It's all fixed up. We can take a run over to Richmond and I'll show you the convent."

Jay felt a sudden rush of affection for him. "You're a good bloke, Dick. Don't ever sell yourself short."

Dick smiled awkwardly. "Knock it off, old man. Come on in and I'll pay this chap and we can get going."

*

He drove in his usual fast and expert fashion and although the car did not have the power of his Jaguar, they reached Richmond in just under an hour.

"The place is on the riverside," he said. "We'll be there soon."

And then what? Jay wondered. What can I do? Can I knock on the door and say, "I demand to see the girl I love. The fifteen-year-old girl I love."

The Mother Superior would probably be very gentle with him, but she would do "what was best for Caroline" in her eyes and that would be to send him away.

"The best for Caroline." Why had such a phrase occurred to him? And then he remembered what Father Costello had once said to him. Would it be better if he never saw her again? He writhed inwardly. If only he knew her state of mind, what she was thinking.

*

The convent was a red brick building, peaceful and secluded behind a high wall. Almost opposite them was a narrow iron-bound gate. After they had been sitting there for a while, it opened and a young girl in school uniform came out.

She passed the car and walked down towards the end of the street and Jay said abruptly, "Let's go, Dick There's nothing I can do here."

Dick turned the car in a tight circle and drove towards the main road. As he slowed at the end of the street waiting his chance to edge out into the main traffic stream, the girl from the convent passed them again and entered a small sweet shop on the corner.

Dick turned off the engine. "Just had an idea, old man. Back in a moment."

He scrambled out of the car, crossed the road and went in the sweet shop.

Jay wondered what he was up to and sat there, waiting for him to return, feeling strangely tired. When Dick came out of the shop, the girl was with him. They stood talking together for a few seconds and then she walked back towards the convent.

Dick opened the door and slipped into his seat. He started the motor and turned into the main road.

After a while he said, "I took a chance then. I stood beside that kid at the counter, bought a packet of cigarettes and then pretended to recognize her blazer. Told her I knew someone who was at her school."

"Go on, for God's sake," Jay said. "Did you ask how Caroline was? Did the girl know?"

"To give it to you straight, she's been very ill. It seems they've all been pretty worried about her."

Jay slumped back into his seat. The world seemed to move in on him for a moment and he shut his eyes and breathed deeply. After a while, he opened them.

"All right, Jay?" Dick said anxiously.

Jay nodded. "Just get me back to camp. I've got to think this thing out."

*

They were easy words to say and foolish for he could see no solution. The night was the longest he had known, worse even than the nights in the cell that had been his home for three months.

He moved uneasily in the narrow bed and despite the bitter cold of the Nissen hut, his body ran with sweat. The other two men in the hut had spoken very little to him and he guessed that Dick must have had a word with them.

He lay in the grey cold of the dawn and smoked cigarette after cigarette and thought about things until his mind spun like a top and he was incapable of coming to any fixed decision.

He didn't go to breakfast and Dick said he would bring him back a cup of tea. He brought more than the tea when he returned.

There was a letter. Jay sat up in bed and sipped his tea and looked at the envelope for a while. It had been re-addressed several times.

"Typical army muck-up," Dick said. "From the date stamp it must have been written about three weeks ago." Jay nodded and finished his tea and Dick said, "It's postmarked Haxby."

Jay tore open the flap. "Old Jonathan must have got someone to write it for him," he said and started to read.

After a while, he dropped it on to the blanket and stared blindly into space.

"Was it from Jonathan?" Dick said.

Jay nodded. "Father Costello wrote it for him. There's one from him also."

Dick read the letters quickly. When he had finished, he looked up, his face serious. "What do you think?"

Jay spoke very quietly, a slight frown on his brow. "In the letter she managed to get out to her grandfather, she says that without me she doesn't want to go on living. As for the priest, he only repeats what he told me months ago. Go away and leave her alone. He thinks she'll get over it."

He pulled the blankets aside and sat on the edge of the bed. "Perhaps he's right. Maybe she would get over it if she had someone to help her, but she hasn't."

Dick stood up and took a few nervous paces across the room. He turned quickly. "There's only one thing to do. You'll have to go and see Margaret Grey. There's nothing on this afternoon. You won't be missed."

Jay frowned. "Do you think she'll see me?"

"There's only one way to find out,' Dick said.

*

When that afternoon he entered the modern office block near the Strand that housed *Fashion and Taste*, he was in a strangely calm state of mind, determined to see Margaret Grey.

He filled in a form stating his business and was asked to wait. He was kept no longer than five minutes. An exquisitely dressed young woman appeared who took him in a lift to the third floor and along a corridor past busy offices that bustled with activity. She knocked on the end door and opened it for him.

It was a beautiful room furnished in contemporary style. Margaret Grey had her desk over against the window and the pale, wintery sun was behind her so that at first glance, she looked quite attractive.

"I thought I might have some difficulty in seeing you," Jay said.

She leaned back in her chair and regarded him calmly. "You look different."

"So I've been told."

"I'd like to make one thing clear before we go any

142

further," she said. "I only asked Colonel Fitzgerald to have a talk with you. Nothing more. What happened was not of my choosing."

"It really doesn't matter." He shrugged. "It's all over now."

She took a cigarette from a silver box and lit it. "What have you come here for?"

He moved past her desk to the window and looked down into the street. He spoke without looking at her. "I'm leaving for Germany within the next few days. I'd like to see Caroline before I go."

"That absolutely impossible." She made an impatient movement. "There's nothing more to say. It was a mistake to see you."

He looked down at her. "I've got to see her. It's a question of her reason, perhaps her life."

Her face was set and hard. "Has she written to you?"

"To her grandfather. A terrible letter. It's worried the old man. He thinks the only person who can straighten her out is me."

"This is really quite absurd. A silly, schoolgirl crush. She'll get over it."

"She seems to be taking her time," Jay said. "In any case, how would you know, Mrs Grey? All your life you've farmed her out on someone else. The only time you ever came running was when you heard she was keeping company with a coloured man."

"Any mother would have done the same," she said. "I was only trying to protect her."

"Protect her or yourself?"

She rose from her chair and took several quick paces across the room. When she turned, she looked rather tired. "I'll let you see Caroline on one condition."

"I'm listening."

"I'll let you see her and talk to her—only for a few minutes, mind you. In return, you must promise not to write to her or to attempt in any way to contact her again. Do you agree?"

"I haven't much choice, have I?" Jay said. "I'll agreed for the period I'm in Germany only. When I come home, we'll see."

For a brief moment they stood in silence gazing at each other and then Margaret Grey sighed and her shoulders sagged. "Very well. I'll agree. I'll bring Caroline to see you just before you leave."

"It should be any day now. Give me your home telephone number and I'll let you know when and where."

There didn't seem anything else to say. She gave him a printed card and he slipped it into his wallet and left.

*

Dick was waiting in a public house just round the corner. Jay gave him the gist of the interview and then ordered a double whisky and swallowed it in one quick gulp. He gazed reflectively into the empty glass, placed it carefully on the bar and said, "Let's get back to camp, Dick."

They did not talk at all during the run back to Aldershot. Jay smoked incessantly and stared out of the window. He sensed Dick's eyes on him and knew that he was worried.

Dick thought he was near breaking-point. But as the thought came to him, he dismissed it. For Jay, the breaking-point had been reached and passed two months before, alone in a ten-foot square cell.

When they reached the camp, Dick went into the N.A.A.F.I. for some cigarettes and Jay returned to their hut on his own. He was lying on the bed staring up at the grimy, fly-specked ceiling when he heard running footsteps outside and Dick's excited voice calling his name.

"It's come, Jay. The movement order. Tomorrow night from Gatwick. It's a special charter flight for families. They're squeezing the four of us in as well."

Jay ran his hands over his face and sat up. Dick was looking at him in a puzzled, uncertain manner. Jay reached into his wallet for the card Margaret Grey had given him.

"Be a good chap and ring this number for me." He handed Dick the card. "Tell Mrs Grey the moment has come sooner than either of us expected."

He lay back against the pillow and listened as Dick's footsteps faded away. In the silence, his thoughts seemed to speak to him, to whisper in his ear : *What are you going to say to her?* He turned over and buried his face in the pillow because there was no answer.

*

And no answer came not even when he stood in the great hall of the airport and gazed through the window at the plane that was to take him away. Nearby were the rest of the passengers mostly women and children, the families of servicemen stationed in Germany. They stood in little groups with clusters of relatives and occasionally, he heard a muffled sob or a small child crying.

Behind him a voice said, "Hello, Jay."

He did not look at her at once. He did not dare. He remained as he was, staring out of the window and then turned very slowly.

She was thin and the rose had fled from her cheeks. A strand of hair straggled over her forehead from beneath the red knitted cap she wore against the cold. Her heavy camel-hair coat looked too big for her.

"Hello, angel," he said and she burst into tears and flung herself into his arms.

He looked across at Margaret Grey standing against the reception desk and then he led Caroline out of the hall into the bitter cold of the night.

They stood by the gate through which he would soon have to pass to his plane and after a while, she was calmer. She managed to laugh when he gave her a cigarette and told her it would do her good.

"Remember the night I came to the sentry box?" she said.

He nodded. "How could I forget? What an impulsive child you were."

Her smile faded. "Not any longer, Jay. What did they do to you in that place? It shows in your eyes."

"That's of no importance," he said. "It's over and done with."

"It was my mother's fault. She was the one who got you into trouble." She gripped the wire mesh of the barrier fiercely. "I hate her. She lost love because she couldn't have it on her own terms. Now she's determined to see that I shan't have it."

"She doesn't understand, that's all," he said.

"What am I going to do without you, Jay?" she said desperately, clutching his coat. "You'll be gone so long."

He pulled her into his arms. "Time has a habit of passing, Caroline. At your age it goes very quickly. I may only be a memory six months from now."

She glared up at him, her face glowing with fire in the sickly yellow light of the arc lamps. "You're the world to me, Jay. Everything good and kind. I shan't ever change." She hugged him hard and snuggled her head against his chest. "At least I'll have your letters to help me."

He said quietly, "But I shan't be writing."

She didn't move at first. After a minute, she raised her face and said, "What did you say?"

"That I shan't be writing."

She started to shake and a little moan escaped from between her lips. He gripped her arms and it took all his strength to hold her still.

"Listen to me, Caroline. It's not my fault. I had to promise. It was the only way I could get to see you. I'll be back, I swear. But I can't write in the meantime. I gave her my word."

People started to pass through the gates towards the plane. He heard footsteps approaching behind him and Dick said, "Sorry, Jay, but we've got to go on board now."

"In a minute," Jay said. "Just give me another minute."

Caroline was quite still now. She was gazing into space at something behind him and there was a vacant expression in her blue eyes.

"Jay?" she said and then again, "Jay?"

A coldness touched the base of his spine. "I'm here, Caroline. I'm here."

Her expression never altered. "Jay, where are you?"

Margaret Grey suddenly appeared in front of him and pulled Caroline gently away. "I'll take her," she said.

He was unable to think, his brain was frozen and numb. He felt a hand pushing him and somehow found himself walking across the tarmac to the plane and Dick was telling him not to worry because it was going to be all right.

He was sitting in a seat by a window and Dick was

fastening the belt for him and then a light flickered on and the plane started to move.

He turned his head quickly and looked out across the tarmac to the gate under the arc lamps, but there was no one there. The plane began to move forward very rapidly.

Chapter Eleven

As the troopship moved in towards Harwich, a steady
rain began to fall. The crowds of servicemen, most of
whom had been waiting since dawn for their first sight
of land, vanished from the decks and went below to
prepare for disembarkation.

Jay buttoned his heavy greatcoat and moved along
the deck towards the bows. He leaned against the rail
and looked towards land.

"It's good to be home, isn't it, old man?" Dick Kerr's
cheerful voice came from behind.

"Yes, it's good to be back," Jay said.

Dick pushed a cigarette at him. "It's been a long
time. Nine months is quite a slice out of anyone's life.
This Aldershot posting's just the thing."

"Another three months and you'll be perfectly free
to go to hell in your own sweet way," Jay said.
"Slightly longer in my case, of course."

They stood side-by-side at the rail for a few
minutes without speaking, watching the busy scene
unfold before them, filled with a disturbed excitement.

"You can smell England," Dick said suddenly. "I
150

never realized it before." He breathed deeply. "My god, but it's wonderful."

"I suppose after all," Jay said, "There is no place quite like it once one gets used to the climate."

"I'm glad you've decided to spend your leave with me," Dick said. "We'll have ourselves a ball during the next few days. Really paint the town red." He laughed suddenly. "I wonder what would have happened to us if we'd never left Greystones. I mean if we'd just gone on taking the course like we were supposed to do in the beginning?"

"Who knows?" Jay said. And after all, who did? His mind slipped back a year to the old house and Haxby and to her. Always to her.

"Remember at first, Jay, before Grant came? It was fine then. Nice and cushy during the day and a pint at The Tall Man with you playing the piano in the evenings?"

Quite suddenly, his voice changed. He said almost sadly, "I wonder what ever became of Tina?"

"You should have written," Jay told him and moved along the rail to get a better view of the dock as they came in.

"How about a last drink before the bar closes?"

"You go ahead. I'll join you in a minute."

Dick nodded and left and Jay walked slowly along to the forward end of the deck and leaned against the rail. He was thinking about Caroline, how she had been and what she had been doing.

It was nine months since their last meeting. Dick

made such an obvious point of never mentioning her that it was almost funny. Jay chuckled and then laughed aloud as the rain increased into a heavy downpour.

Only England could give the returning traveller such a welcome and yet the very smell of the land, blown through the rain, was enough to cheer the heart. He decided after all, to join Dick at the bar and went below.

*

Before commencing their leave it was necessary for them first to report to their new unit. The rest of the morning passed quickly. They entrained for London and a truck took them straight from Liverpool Street Station to Aldershot. For once the army excelled itself and in a little over two hours, they were boarding a London train at Aldershot Station.

They took a taxi to Dick's house in St John's Wood and left their luggage there. The Jaguar was in the garage, serviced and ready for use and in a few minutes, they were driving into the West End.

"Just like old times," Dick said as they moved through the heavy traffic.

Jay considered the point. How could it be like old times without Caroline? He wondered where she was, how far away? Somehow, he was going to see her, but there was his promise to Margaret Grey to consider. He was still bound by that. He knew that he would have to see *her* first.

"We'll have a damned good meal and a decent bottle of wine with it," Dick said. "The pubs should be opening by then and we can have a few drinks. How's that sound?"

"Wonderful," Jay said and meant it.

*

They dined at a restaurant in Soho and afterwards had their drinks. In fact they had several. The world began to expand for Jay, people became larger, voices louder. There was no problem he could not face and solve on his own two feet. He came to that decision in a quiet corner of a noisy public bar in Chelsea.

"When are you going to see your professor?" Dick said. Jay had received the tentative offer of an assistant lectureship at London University mainly on the strength of his book.

Jay emptied his glass. "That can wait. There's something much more important to settle." He thrust a cigarette packet under Dick's nose, spilling half the contents on the table. "Sorry, I think I'm a trifle cut."

Dick was quite sober. He gathered the spilled cigarettes with one hand and said, without looking up, "And what have you to do that's so important?"

Jay lit his cigarette with a shaking hand. "Remember Caroline? My Caroline?"

Dick's smile was pasted into place. "Hell, I thought you'd forgotten. It's been a long time. Too long to go turning over old stones."

"That's just where you're wrong."

Dick waved his hand for the waiter. "What you need is another one."

He ordered two drinks. When he turned his head, Jay was smiling at him, holding out a small white card between his fingers.

"Remember this? Margaret Grey gave it to me when I called to see her that day. When you phoned her for me, you used it to get her home number. I've kept it all this time. Tonight, I intend to return it."

Dick pushed a drink across. "Come on, down the hatch. Why spoil a good night remembering unpleasantness?"

Jay leaned across the table. "You don't want me to go and see her do you?"

Dick laughed and his smile slipped a little. "It's just that she might make trouble for you, Jay. You've got the chance of a good job in a leading university. The first step towards the kind of life you've always wanted. Why start trouble with a woman who may possibly cause you a great deal of harm?"

"She can't harm me, now or ever. Her daughter isn't fifteen any longer."

"You're drunk. How can you possibly speak to her in that condition?"

Jay emptied his glass. "Is that your only objection?"

"Of course," Dick said hurriedly.

"Then let's get going." Jay slammed the glass down on the table so that it smashed into several pieces and blood spurted from a gash in his hand.

People were staring and for a moment there was

154

silence followed by a burst of conversation as the incident was discussed and then dismissed.

"All right, old man. We'll go now."

He nodded to the waiter who was forcing his way through the crowd towards them and tossed a couple of pound notes on to the table. He took Jay firmly by the elbow and pushed him outside.

*

It was a brilliant night with a full moon bathing the London scene in its hard, white light. The Jaguar rolled along the quiet Chelsea streets and Jay laid back his head and tried to relax.

"Are you still bent on seeing her?" Dick said.

Jay fumbled in his pocket and pulled out the white card. "Here's the address—something Mews, I think. Just get me there, Dick."

He closed his eyes, fought against the drink that clouded his brain. The car moved through the night and the cold air stung his face and he tried to remember other nights and what they had meant to him, and then he thought of Caroline and all doubts fled.

The car braked, turned into a side street and halted.

"This is it, old man," Dick said as he switched off the engine. "I'll wait for you here."

Jay stood on the pavement and swayed a little as he looked at the house. A wrought-iron lamp was suspended above the door. He could have sworn it was swinging from side-to-side.

He mounted the steps to the door and pressed the bell-push. A peal of melodious chimes sounded inside and after a while, footsteps approached. The door opened and a maid appeared. A wary expression came into her eyes.

"I'd like a word with Mrs Grey."

"I'm sorry, sir, she left strict instructions not to be disturbed tonight."

He stepped across the threshold and gently pushed her before him. "I think she'll see *me*," he said.

The maid backed away in alarm. He moved forward again and she hurriedly stood to one side. There was a door beyond and he could hear the noise of a typewriter. He turned the knob and went in.

*

Margaret Grey was sitting at a small table by the fire, a typewriter before her, a pile of manuscripts on the floor. The only illumination came from a small desk-lamp.

"What is it, Jean?" she said without looking up.

"I thought I might have some difficulty in seeing you," Jay said and by some strange quirk of memory, remembered that he had used exactly those words when he had gone to her office that day that seemed so long ago.

She sat behind the typewriter, looking at him as if he were a ghost. Her face had gone white and two small spots began to glow, one in either cheek.

"What do you want?" she whispered.

Her voice seemed to come across water and he found difficulty in keeping her in focus. He took a deep breath and said, "I'm back and I've every intention of seeing Caroline again if she wants to see me. I thought I'd let you know."

Her sigh seemed to echo away through the silent spaces of eternity. "I'm afraid that won't be possible. Caroline is dead."

He raised his hands as if to protect himself from a physical blow and saw to his surprise, that one of them was covered in blood. That blood had seeped into his sleeve.

Oh, yes, the glass, he thought. I broke the glass in the bar. The shadows moved in from the four corners of the room with a terrible weightless pressure. The darkness moved in and moved out and after a while, he broke through to the surface and found himself sitting in a chair beside the table.

She was holding a glass to his lips. He coughed as the brandy burned the back of his throat, and he managed to get her in focus again.

He caught her arm and pulled her close. "How did it happen?"

"There was an accident," she said. "Does it matter now?"

Her face was still very white and there was an unnatural calmness about her. He shivered as if somewhere, someone had walked over his grave, relaxed his grip on her arm and stood up.

He noticed he had bloodied the sleeve of her

dress and carefully wiped his hand on his battledress blouse.

"A little more love," he said. "A little more understanding. That's all she needed, Mrs Grey. What did you give her?"

"And you?" she said. "Were you so immaculate in this business? Were you really in love with Caroline or with the idea that she could love someone like you?"

He took a step backwards, horror on his face. "What are you trying to say?"

"A hard fact of life I've learned during the past few months," she said. "That no one can ever honestly say where a thing begins or ends."

There was something close to pity in her eyes.

He turned and lurched into the corridor, wrenched open the front door and fled into the street. He heard Dick call anxiously and he rushed past the car without stopping.

At the end of the street there was a church and he opened a gate and sought sanctuary amongst the swaying tombstones. His stomach heaved and he dropped to his knees and was sick.

Presently, he got up wearily, sat on the edge of a marble tomb and lit a cigarette with shaking hands. The smoke bit into his throat and he tried to unfreeze his mind so that he could think.

She had gone and the terrible thing was that he was to blame. He had sown the seeds of their tragedy and she had been the one to suffer. Every single human action, however small, was like a stone dropped into a pond and the ripples moved out to unknown shores.

He heard the jarring creak of the gate as it was pushed open and Dick moved between the tombstones towards him. "You all right, Jay?"

"She's dead, Dick. Caroline's dead."

"I know," Dick said. "I've known for a long time."

For some strange reason, Jay felt no particular surprise. "How did you find out?"

"Jonathan Grey sent a letter to me. It was a long time ago, just after we got to Berlin. He left it open to my judgement whether or not to tell you. I didn't think it was wise at that time."

"How could you let me live all this time without knowing?"

"God help me, Jay, it was for your own good."

"That's what everyone said to Caroline. Look where it got her."

Jay scrambled to his feet, swaying slightly as the drink started to take control again. "Give me the car keys. I'm going to drive North to see Jonathan."

"You can't, Jay. You're in no condition to go anywhere."

"I'm warning you. I want that key. If you won't give it to me, I'll take it."

Dick backed away. "You're drunk, Jay. Come and lie down for a while."

Jay swung his right fist in a wide arc. He missed completely and fell flat on his face. As he started to get up he heard Dick say, "Sorry, old man."

Something hit him under his left ear and coloured lights exploded inside his head.

*

He was lying on a divan with a blanket over him. He looked at the ceiling for quite some time before turning his head to see where he was.

The room was in semi-darkness and Dick was sitting beside a bright fire under a shaded lamp. A cigarette smouldered between his lips and he held a half-empty glass in his hand.

Jay felt strangely calm and quite sober. "What did you hit me with?" he said quietly and swung his legs to the floor.

Dick crossed the room quickly. "Just my fist. Sorry, but you were off your head."

Jay nodded. "You did the best thing. "There was a tightness behind his eyes. "Tell me, did Jonathan give you any details in that letter?"

Dick moved over to the sideboard and poured a couple of drinks." He just said that she was dead and ask me to do what I thought was best. Here, drink this. It'll do you good."

"What time is it?"

"Just after one a.m. You were out a long time."

Jay stood up and groaned as a band of iron settled around his head. "I'll have to go, Dick. I must find out what happened. Jonathan will tell me."

"Do you want me to come with you?"

"I'd rather be on my own."

"I'll get the Jaguar out for you." Dick put down his glass and left the room.

Jay dressed quickly and when he heard the car engine, went into the hall and let himself out. It was a cold night with a thick hoar frost coating everything.

Dick got out of the car and said, "Better wear this. It's got a sheepskin lining. You'll find it cold on the Great North Road tonight."

Jay pulled on the heavy coat and buttoned it closely about his neck. He slipped behind the wheel and checked the controls.

In the diffused light from the lamp above the door, Dick was pale and drawn. They looked at each other for several moments, but for some strange reason, there did not seem anything to say.

Jay made a tiny gesture of finality with one hand and let the Jaguar into gear. Sweeping into the main road with a surge of power, he raced through the cold darkness northwards.

Chapter Twelve

There was little traffic about and he was alone with his thoughts and the steady hum of the engine. He had discovered, soon after starting, that his right hand was heavily bandaged and remembered the broken glass, realizing that Dick must have given him first-aid when he was unconscious. The hand gave him a certain amount of pain and he rested it lightly on the steering wheel, using his left as much as possible.

The moon was still full and there were no clouds in the sky. It was cold and the car skidded on the corners because of the frost, but mainly because he was driving too fast.

He wanted to get to Haxby as soon as possible. He wanted to see old Jonathan to find out what had happened. At the back of his mind, pushed well down into the subconscious because he didn't wish to think about it, was the horrible thought that perhaps she had found her own way out.

He remembered the first evening they had spent together and how he had not recognized her when she walked across the road because she looked so different.

That evening at the concert, that very first evening

had shown him what was to come. He should have stopped then and there. He should have told her the whole thing was out of the question. But the terrible thing was that he had not. That meant quite simply, that he and he alone, was responsible for all that had happened since.

But how could I have left her? he asked himself. She was so lonely. Except for Jonathan, she had nobody. The whole affair had been complicated from the start. He had been necessary to her because she so desperately needed someone to whom she could give her own love. A tightness tugged at his throat and he swallowed hard.

He tried to remember everything from the beginning. Every little detail. The things she had said, the clothes she had worn.

Suddenly and for no apparent reason, he remembered the candlelight party and Turner with his secret of happiness. Be happy for the moment and don't think of tomorrow. A moment's happiness is all happiness. Was that what he had said?

Jay laughed bitterly, wishing he could meet Turner again to tell him how wrong he had been. How sterile, how hopeless. Did Turner know that when a woman died part of a man could die with her? But then he was like so many people. Secure in a world of his own creating, bound by his own philosophy, believing what he wished to believe.

The engine started to falter. He glanced at the petrol gauge and saw that the tank was still half-full. As the car lost speed, he came to the top of a hill and saw the lights of an all-night garage below.

He coasted down the hill and drew in beside the pumps. A mechanic came out of the small office yawning and Jay said, "Looks like a petrol stoppage. Check it, will you?" He noticed a small café standing at the back of the car park. "I'll be in there."

The mechanic nodded and he walked across the gravel stiffly as the blood began to circulate in his cramped legs.

The café was warm and smelt of tea and stale cigarette smoke. It was completely deserted and he had to bang on the counter for a minute or two until a young blonde emerged from the kitchen to serve him.

She gave him tea in a chipped mug and then sullenly disappeared back into the kitchen. He sat on a high stool at the counter and sipped the tea, regarding himself in the mirror.

His cheeks were sunken, the skin stretched tightly over the bones, but it was the look in the eyes that frightened him. He lit a cigarette, puffed at it nervously and then realized he was banging his right hand on the counter.

Blood was seeping through the bandage and he became aware that his hand was hurting him—hurting him a lot. I should see a doctor, he thought. It probably needs stitching. He got up from the stool and nervously walked across the room and looked out through the glass door into the dark. As he turned he saw the juke box standing in the corner.

He stood for several moments just looking at it, remembering that first night with Caroline when they had ended up at the roadside café with the fruit machines and the juke box.

He slipped a coin into the slot. After a while, the record he had selected at random started to play. It was something slow and sentimental and straight off the Hit Parade.

All he knew, as the sadness surged through him, was that last time he'd had Caroline to dance with and now he was on his own. He was on his own for good.

*

He wrenched open the door and went out into the night. The mechanic was walking towards him. "It's okay now, mate. Just a bit of dirt in the pump."

"Fill her up quickly," Jay said. "I'm in a hurry."

He sat in the car and waited and the mechanic leaned in the off-side window and said, "She took four, that'll be thirty bob altogether."

Jay pushed a couple of pound notes into the man's hand and took the Jaguar away in a burst of speed without waiting for his change.

*

He drove recklessly and very fast, completely ignoring all speed limits. Dawn began to stain the sky and when morning came, it was grey and sombre with heavy rain clouds moving across his path. It was shortly after seven when he reached the Rainford bypass. Skirting the city, he finally turned into the road to Haxby.

Ten minutes later, he saw the chimneys of Caroline's house pushing up through the trees. He changed down, swung the car through the gate and finally stopped at the bottom of the steps leading up to the front door.

He jumped out of the car and halted, one foot on the bottom step. Jonathan Grey was standing in the garden, his massive, white-topped head turned towards the house. Jay went forward and then he saw Digby the Labrador.

The dog growled and stood quite still, ears cocked. The growl changed to a whine of pleasure and his tail wagging, he scampered across the lawn, and jumped up to meet Jay's welcoming hand.

"Hello, Jay," Jonathan Grey said.

"How did you know?"

"Dick phoned three or four hours ago. You must be tired."

Jay realized that he was. More tired than he had ever been. His eyes felt gritty and his back ached and the wound in his hand throbbed painfully. He followed Jonathan Grey into the house and they went into the kitchen.

"I'll make some coffee," the old man said.

"I can do it, sir."

"No need, my boy. I'm quite an expert in the kitchen these days."

It's just the same, Jay thought as he looked round the kitchen. Nothing changed. He remembered how he had always insisted on drying for her when she washed the dishes, and the late-night meals she would cook for him with the house sleeping and just the two of them alone and cosy in the kitchen. And then the door had opened early one morning and Margaret Grey had walked in.

"Here you are, my boy." Jonathan Grey was holding out a cup of coffee.

Jay sipped it gratefully. As life began to stir in him again he said, "Doesn't Mrs Brown come any more?"

The old man shook his head. "I have a very nice woman from the outskirts of Rainford, but she doesn't get here until nine."

Jay swallowed some more coffee and said, "How did it happen? I want to know. I want to know every detail. Don't miss anything out."

The old man poured himself another cup of coffee with a sure hand. "Have you seen Margaret?"

"She told me it was an accident?"

The old man nodded. "Then she told you the truth."

"I prefer to judge for myself. How did she die?"

"She was drowned. And she didn't commit suicide, if that's what you're thinking."

"Tell me what happened?" Jay said in a whisper.

"It must have been about a month after you left for Germany—March, I think. She'd been very ill indeed. When she arrived here she was in a state of acute depression."

"She did leave her mother, then?"

"Not officially. Margaret had gone to America for a

couple of weeks. Some business connected with the magazine. Caroline had been living with her and was left in the charge of a trained nurse. Apparently, she just walked out one day, got on a train and came up here. Unfortunately, she ran out of money. She wasn't thinking straight or she could have got a taxi from the station and paid at this end. She got a bus to the edge of Rainford and walked the rest of the way. It was raining and bitterly cold. She arrived in a state of complete collapse. I called a doctor and he diagnosed pneumonia."

"Oh, my God," Jay breathed, remembering the first time he had met her. What had he said? *Not a pleasant way to leave the world—not for one so young, anyhow.*

Old Jonathan continued calmly, "We discovered she was missing from her bed one morning. Of course I notified the police because she'd been delirious the night before and in a high fever. They found her in the lake at Rainford Park. How she ever got there, God only knows. She was floating in the water just under the jetty. They decided she must have leaned on the rail, it broke and she fell in. The coroner's verdict was mis-adventure."

This is how it ends, Jay thought. A fine, lovely girl, full of life and hope and love, choked in the dark waters.

"It was my fault, you know, sir. I'm to blame."

Jonathan Grey shook his head and said calmly, "I don't think so."

"It was an impossible situation from the beginning. I knew that. I'd had twenty-three years to learn the hard way, Caroline didn't realize how cruel life can be."

"And what about her mother?"

"She did what she thought was for the best, according to her own lights. I was the one that started the chain reaction."

Jonathan Grey shook his head. "There's no beginning, no end to anything, Jay. That's something you learn as you get older. We're all guilty from the moment we're born."

Jay carried his cup over to the sink and rinsed it. "Where is she buried?"

"In Haxby at the church. Why don't you call on Father Costello? He'd like to see you, I know."

Jay nodded slowly and said as he opened the door, "I don't know if I'll be seeing you again."

Jonathan Grey smiled gently. "I think so, Jay. I think so."

"It's a dirty world, isn't it?"

"Not the world, my boy. Just the people in it. But not always."

Jay closed the door, walked round to the front of the house and drove away quickly. So now he knew. And there was no answer.

*

He pulled up at the church just as the rain began to

fall. He ignored it and walked across to the cemetery. It took him a good half-hour to find her grave. When he did, he sat on a nearby tomb in the rain and looked at the headstone for a long time.

"CAROLINE GREY SIXTEEN YEARS"

These were the only words that seemed to make sense and yet there was still no answer for him.

He moved through the ageing grave stones back towards the church, went inside and sat down at the back. It was very still and he was alone with the winking candles and the images.

For a moment, time seemed to have no meaning and he turned his head and looked beside him, but he was quite alone. There was nothing for him here. Nothing at all.

Behind him, the door banged, there was a blast of cold air and the candles fluttered wildly. Someone moved along the aisle and passed him. Jay stood up and edged out quietly. He stumbled against a chair and the other stopped and said, "Good morning." It was Father Costello.

"Good morning, Father," Jay said and turned to go.

"One moment please." The priest stepped forward quickly. "Jay," he said. "Jay Williams."

Suddenly, Jay was aware that his head was hurting and that his hand felt as if red-hot nails were being hammered into it. The smell of the incense was overpowering and he felt curiously light-headed and some-how, outside himself.

"I've got to go, Father," he said. "Sorry I can't stay, but I haven't got much time."

The priest caught hold of his sleeve. "Jay, I must talk to you."

Jay pulled away sharply. He moved to the door and ran out into the pouring rain. A moment later, he drove recklessly away.

*

There was only one place to go. It had been raining the first time he had gone there, it was raining now. That must mean something, but he couldn't think what.

It didn't take him long to get to Rainford and he took the road he had taken that first day he had gone to the park. He left the Jaguar by the museum and walked down through the trees to the lake.

It was raining very hard now and by the time he reached the jetty, it had begun to soak through the shoulders of the heavy coat Dick had given him that morning. Was it only that morning? Standing at the end of the jetty, it seemed longer ago than that first day when he and Caroline had stood there.

He noticed that one piece of wood in the rail was different from the others, that obviously it had been inserted more recently. It came to him that he was standing where she had stood that morning, that he was touching the very place she had touched before the rotten wood had given way and she had fallen down to the icy water.

He stood looking out across the lake as if listening for something and then nodded his head several times as though in confirmation of some secret, hidden decision.

He pulled a crumpled packet of cigarettes from his pocket. As he extracted one he noticed that blood was seeping through the bandage on his hand again and yet he could feel pain no longer. He felt strangely at peace and he took out a match, lit the cigarette and said calmly, "When I have finished this cigarette, I shall jump in."

The rain was cold and bitter as death and by now, had drenched his head and shoulders. He held the cigarette cupped in his left hand and drew on it unsteadily a couple of times. The rain, trickling through his fingers, soaked the paper and the cigarette burst and yellow tobacco spilled out over his hand.

He gazed at it sadly and then tilted his hand sideways and the rain washed the remnants of the tobacco away, down through the air to the dark water.

He took a deep breath and put a hand on the rail. Somewhere, high in the sky, a seagull whirled and cried harshly.

"That's what I'd like to be when I die—a seagull flying in the rain over the water." Her voice still sounded in his ear, dimly like a faint echo in an old room.

He began to cry, terribly and agonizingly. He was

not crying for Caroline alone. He was crying for himself. He was also crying for the world.

Sobbing, he turned and walked along the jetty. The seagull cried eerily as it dipped over his head and fled through the grey rain.

TO CATCH A KING

Harry Patterson

His previous bestsellers include *The Eagle has Landed*, *The Valhalla Exchange* and *Storm Warning*. Now Harry Patterson (alias Jack Higgins) has transformed the facts of history into his most compelling thriller to date.

July 1940. While the world awaits the invasion of England, a plot unfolds in Lisbon that could change the course of the war. Its instigator: Adolf Hitler. Its target: the Duke of Windsor. Its aim: to catch a king. Only one man could have conceived of so daring, so deadly a plot. Only the maddest moments of history could have made it possible.

£1.60

THE VALHALLA EXCHANGE

Harry Patterson

Fact!
Dawn April 30th 1945. Russian radar reports a light aircraft leaving one of the last strongholds in besieged Berlin – passengers and destination unknown.

Fiction?
In a concret bunker beneath the burning city, Reichsleiter Martin Bormann assembles a crack team to fly him out of a tightening Soviet ring around the capital. Objective – the medieval fortress of Arlberg where a group of VIP prisoners are to be used as bargaining counters in the epic struggle to come.

'Patterson is in his element here, with lots of fast, fierce fighting, subterfuge and inside betrayals.'
Publishers Weekly

£1.50

SAD WIND FROM THE SEA

Harry Patterson

Hagan was thinking that he had finally run out of luck – that he had lost everything and had nothing left to lose – when he heard a woman scream. She was young, she was beautiful, and she shouldn't have been on the waterfront of Macao at three in the morning. Hagan knew immediately that the girl meant trouble – big trouble. But as Hagan himself said, 'I love trouble, angel. It makes life so much more exciting.'

This time, however, Hagan will find himself in more trouble than even he is used to as the strange Eurasian beauty leads him into a desperate treasure hunt that takes him into the heart of Red China.

£1.60